To Jennie,
Thanks so much
for helping us.

Terry R. King

DEATHLY GIFTED

BLACK PROPHECIES SERIES

TERRY R. KING

iUniverse®

DEATHLY GIFTED
BLACK PROPHECIES SERIES

Edited by Lindsey Schwimmer and Leah Tielke

iUniverse books may be ordered through booksellers or by contacting:

iUniverse
1663 Liberty Drive
Bloomington, IN 47403
www.iuniverse.com
844-349-9409

ISBN: 978-1-6632-5307-1 (sc)
ISBN: 978-1-6632-5309-5 (hc)
ISBN: 978-1-6632-5308-8 (e)

Library of Congress Control Number: 2023908519

Print information available on the last page.

iUniverse rev. date: 05/15/2023

To my wife and daughters. You gave me the encouragement to finally start this. Thank you, and I love you!

CHAPTER 1

FIRST DEATH HOUSE

ROBERT FOUND THE HOUSE AGAIN. HE DROVE BY IT ONCE, THEN again, just to get a feel for it. The houses in this area were spaced far apart, with big yards and lots of mature trees surrounding them. He pulled his Jeep into the long gravel driveway and parked some distance from the house, beneath one of the large shade trees. He got out of his Jeep to begin his visit to this house.

He was here because of a phone call from a man named Samuel White. Someone had been killing young women in Pennsylvania, Mr. White's daughter among them. The police had dropped the investigation after their suspect, a drug addict, committed suicide. Mr. White believed the police had the wrong suspect all along and the killer was still out there. That was why he and the other families of the deceased had used a private detective to find and hire Robert. Robert had something the police didn't: a paranormal gift that allowed him to see, smell, hear, and sense the emotions from traumatic events of the past—events that often-included death or, in this case, murder.

Autumn had always been Robert's favorite season—today it was very sunny and warm, with just a gentle breeze and an occasional gust that blew the tree limbs and dried maple leaves about. His senses were now on high alert.

Unlike the other houses that surrounded this one, the grass and weeds were overgrown in the vast yard, which hadn't been mowed in years. This house had to be abandoned. The house was a large two-story white frame with a wraparound front porch.

It seemed to be very old, maybe mid to late 1800s, but in pretty good condition still. Robert wondered how long it had been vacant and why it wasn't for sale. Without any previous knowledge of the house, he had no idea how much good or evil had occurred here either. He sensed that large happy families had lived here years to decades earlier.

Robert could see a tree on the left side where a swing had hung. Parts of the rope remained, but the seat was long gone. There was still a void in the grass of the dirt path beneath the swing where the kids had dragged their feet.

Farther back toward the rear of the house, Robert could see the remains of a tree house, with a small red flag that moved gently in the light breeze. The tree house was breaking down, and parts of the wood had fallen to the ground beneath. Now-dilapidated boards nailed to the tree had provided steps to the landing, and a long rope with occasional knots tied along its length had given the kids a way to climb up too.

From this distance, Robert could sense good or happy feelings, laughing children and adults. Beneath that, he could sense some sadness and spotty darker energy, like dread, anger, and even hate which he'd expected.

When Robert heard these voices, the words were usually not very clear. Most of the time, they sound muffled and mumbled, like they were far away—or like when you're in an apartment and you can hear people talking and laughing in an adjoining unit. He usually couldn't understand exactly what they were saying, but he could recognize the emotions and tell whether the people involved were male or female, young or very old. When he heard the arguments and anger, though, oftentimes that was clearer.

Robert turned and walked closer to the house and could see plants and weeds around it, with large overgrown bushes and small spotty patches of flowers—flowers that a mother had planted on her knees with a small shovel, probably with her daughter's help.

They were now long neglected. The blooms had fallen off, and only bare stems remained. The word *tulips* popped into Robert's thoughts. He was sure that at a different time of the year it would still look much prettier.

He walked up the steps to the porch and headed to the front door, approaching slowly to immerse himself in this place's past. The laughter from the yard began to seem more strangled and faded. The only information shared with Robert about this house was that a murder had been committed on the first floor.

He could now sense the impending darkness getting worse as a low throbbing emanated from the house. Unfortunately, bad feelings seemed to far outweigh the good. Like violence on the six o'clock news. The reality was that bad news sold better than good news, which further confirmed to Robert that evil outweighed good in this world.

Negative energy has power.

At the front door, Robert took hold of the doorknob. The door was latched but not locked. He entered, and at first, he continued to hear the wind blowing and the leaves rustling about on the front porch. The laughter and happiness he had sensed outside now began to fade. He left the front door open and walked to the center of the foyer. There was no furniture present—anywhere. He felt like the house had been empty for a long time.

He could see that there were nice plank wood floors throughout, with beautiful wood trim along the walls. The paint color had faded, and the wallpaper was mostly intact, but some of the edges were curled. The staircase still appeared sturdy. He looked into the dining room to the right and could see empty beer cans and trash from either a vagrant trespassing or teenagers partying. No—he had a feeling it had been a vagrant. There were some newspapers folded up by the wall too, and the trash seemed like it had been neatly piled. The man had lived here for some time before moving on and was tidy and neat with his temporary space in the house.

Robert closed his eyes and spread his arms out to immerse himself in the sensations around him. He had no idea how much time passed until he descended to become part of it. This was the space he needed to be in to enter his vision. All the sounds of birds chirping and leaves rattling outside disappeared as he entered the vision.

Once he reopened his eyes, the bright sunshine of the day had dimmed, and he felt he was now in the evening on which this young woman had died. When he tuned in to a bad vision, all ambient sounds, lights, and realities disappeared. He tuned into different bad experiences that had occurred around him. Again, like the news, the bad experiences dominated the good. Unfortunately, he was here for a bad or evil experience.

He began to hear distant, muffled yelling, arguing, and crying from several different women and children's voices and an occasional male shouting. It was evident the sounds had been trapped here over a long period of time. Robert longed to go back outside and feel the happiness, but he was here to witness the anger and hatred that was stuck inside this house and one moment in particular. Then there was a moment of eerie silence. The angry family sounds even vanished. The deeper he got into the vision, the darker or eviler it became. It continued until it was broken by a long, loud, agonizing scream that seemed to reverberate throughout this old house.

Then he could hear heavy breathing or gasping and a struggle from within the next room. As he walked through the archway into what looked to be an old living room, he could smell what he thought was a horrible case of body odor, or like someone shit their pants, and turned to see semitransparent images of a pretty young woman and a large bulky dark man near the far end of the room.

She had pale skin and thin straight brown hair, and she stared around with striking blue eyes as she gasped frantically in shock and pain. Her left eye had a large bruise; her lip was bleeding, probably from having been struck; and she had a round bloody place on the side of her head. Robert noticed a sledgehammer on a table close to them with blood on the hammerhead. The killer had dark hair, a scraggly beard, and a wide face. He looked like a disgruntled lumberjack, with a long-sleeved flannel shirt, jeans, and dried muddy boots.

With his large gloved left hand, the man held the woman by her throat. She struck at him with her hands and fists and tried to kick him with her small feet. She was slim and petite and she was having no impact on him. Then Robert noticed the killer holding the handle of a knife that he had already inserted into her abdomen below her left breast.

He withdrew the knife and inserted it into the neckline of her dress and then sliced it down to her groin, opening her dress wide open, exposing her bra and panties and smooth pale stomach.

Her eyes rolled over to look at him, and she shouted, "Please don't kill me!"

The man had his back to Robert at first, but he turned his head slightly, revealing a sinister smiling face with yellowed teeth. A couple of teeth were missing, and the smile unnerved Robert.

The man stepped to the side, and Robert could see him take his right hand and slide the long blade of the knife back into the woman's abdomen between her ribs. His leather gloves would prevent fingerprints.

She moaned loudly from the pain. Robert thought he could actually hear the metal scraping her bones and saw her blood spurt out, spilling over the blade, covering the man's gloved hand before streaming to the floor. Even though this had already occurred, Robert felt so horrible that this was happening to this young woman.

Robert teared up and was soon crying. He really wanted to save her from such an awful death but couldn't. At that moment, he wasn't sure he could continue to see these types of deaths, even though he knew it would help the families. The woman kept crying and moaning, and the killer began laughing and looking from the knife to her face. He tilted his head back and forth, staring at her madly, concentrating on how she was responding to what he was doing to her.

He almost completely removed the knife and then rapidly shoved it back in, in a different direction. Robert thought the knife caught on a bone for a moment before sliding the rest of the way in.

"No!" Robert yelled. "Don't do that! Please stop!"

The killer was manic in his actions. Suddenly he moved to her right side and stumbled, and at that moment, the woman lunged forward, hoping she might get away, and pulled loose from the killer. He attempted to regain his grip on her, and she tried to stumble away. He lost his hold on her for a moment.

He groaned loudly and yelled, "You fucking bitch! You are mine!"

She was moving toward Robert, and he thought for a moment she might get away. She reached out as though she were reaching for him as he spontaneously stepped aside. Her ghostly image was so close to him he could have reached out and touched her. She had a look of abject terror on her face and still had the large knife protruding from her side.

She almost reached the doorway before the killer caught up with her, grabbing her hair and pulling her backward tightly. He looped his hand in her hair and continued to pull her back in the room. She again screamed loudly and broke down crying. It had no impact on the killer.

He quickly removed the knife, moved it to her pretty bare neck, and dragged the blade across it, away from him, leaving a light blood trail in its wake. The killer then slowly pulled the blade back toward him and forced the knife deeper, opening a larger gash.

Blood began flowing rapidly down her neck and body, following the knife across the width of the slice. At this point, her eyes and mouth were wide open, but she seemed to simply stare into space. Her mouth was opening and closing like a fish gasping for air. She would soon be dead.

Robert hoped her pain was gone now. The killer stared into her eyes and grinned. He moved his face close to hers and sniffed deeply as if he were trying to smell her death. He then slowly licked the side of her face. He kept staring into her eyes. Her focus soon slipped from her eyes, though he was trying to look into them and watch her die.

She was wearing a pretty silver St. Christopher's pendant on a silver chain. The man quickly yanked the necklace off and stuck his new trophy in his pocket. He had to be holding her erect at this point, because she certainly couldn't have been standing on her own. She was lovely, and while the dress had been an attractive pale blue, it was now absorbing the flowing dark red blood. He quickly sliced her front from her neck to her panties, leaving another blood trail.

He reached the very sharp knife behind her and sliced her hair between his hand and her head, cleanly cutting the locks in two. She collapsed backward and fell in her own blood with a soft thump. He dropped most of the hair on her but put some in one of his pockets. He looked at her on the floor and turned with a huge smile on his face. His yellowed teeth were bloodstained, and so were his lips and chin.

He gazed at his work for a couple of minutes, and before Robert could react, the killer turned, grabbed the hammer off the table, and walked right through Robert and out the doorway. Robert was in shock for a moment. It felt like a cold, odorous mist had washed through him when the killer walked through him. When he turned to look at the woman who had just been murdered, her eyes were still wide open, and she seemed to be staring at him. Her mouth was no longer moving, and she started fading. Robert began coming out of this murder vision. He then slowly looked around the rest of the house, even upstairs, for any further clues, but he saw nothing else. Of course the police had gathered any evidence that may have been here.

He returned to the foyer, where he looked around again, still horrified. He slowly walked out the door, down the porch steps, and into the yard. The vision was completely gone, and he now returned to the beautiful early afternoon outside, but this grisly murder vision made the day feel stained now. About halfway to his Jeep, he stopped to turn around and once again look at the house.

The house did not seem happy anymore, even though it had returned to the happier, more family-positive aura that it had taken on before he entered. It was no longer the same. He got in his Jeep and sat there for a few minutes, collecting his thoughts and unwinding from the horrific vision, before taking some notes and starting the engine. He turned around in the driveway, continuing to look at and listen to the house. He left and began the drive up the long gravel driveway and then down the country road heading towards the hotel.

CHAPTER 2

ROBERT ANDERSON

His name was Robert Anderson. He was from Cincinnati, Ohio. He felt he'd had a relatively normal family life growing up. His family consisted of his mother and father and twin sisters. They'd loved going to Graeter's Ice Cream, Skyline Chili, and LaRosa's pizza as a family pretty often.

Robert's maternal grandmother had lived with them for a while, and she'd often talked about having a "gift," or a sight for unusual or unnatural things. Grandma used to live with Grandpa and Robert's mother and her siblings in a small coal-mining town in southern Kentucky, long since abandoned since the mining stopped.

Grandma had said, "When I was much younger, I used to see smoky, moving black figures around the town where I lived. Not everyone saw them like I did." Today they might call that a *shadow figure*. It seemed to appear randomly. The way Robert understood it, shadow figures were supposed to be bad spirits. He believed a bad spirit came from a bad person. He hadn't seen one yet.

She had also talked about a woman in a flowing white dress who seemed to glow and would appear at a neighbor's gate over and over again.

He believed that was a residual haunting of a woman who had died there and was just repeating some of the final moments of her life. Grandma also talked of having deceased people's spirits visiting her at times.

To her it all seemed normal. Back then, things like that seemed much more acceptable. Unlike today, there weren't a lot of people around telling you these things couldn't be true.

Robert had the so-called gift too. He'd inherited it in his DNA, you might say. His paranormal senses weren't very strong when he was younger. He remembered occasionally noticing odd sounds, smells, and semitransparent people from time to time, but it was fairly dormant until he was sixteen. At that time, he was involved in a car wreck that made it stronger—or fully activate. He soon discovered it wasn't easy to be normal with his sort of gift. There was no off switch for it. It was on all the time and unpredictable.

Robert's life changed in an instant one day. It was typical for Robert and his friends to get out and drive around when they didn't have anything else to do. Robert didn't have his license or a car yet. It was rainy that day and his friend Jimmy was driving and spun his wheels and slid. Robert yelled at him, "Hey, dude, take it easy!" Jimmy broke up laughing at him. Robert was just more cautious. They were about to stop for LaRosa's pizza.

Just ahead, there was an overpass, with a small right turn just before they went under the street above. When they hit the small turn, Jimmy punched it, and his car slid sideways on the rainy street. Jimmy thought he had it straightened out when it continued to slide and ran into the corner of a concrete wall right before the overpass.

The last thing Robert remembered thinking was *Oh shit! We're going to hit!* He saw the wall getting closer to his door, and as he closed his eyes, the impact seemed incredible as it crushed the metal door and sent glass flying everywhere. He didn't remember his head hitting the corner of the concrete wall. He was knocked unconscious at that moment. Jimmy managed to pull away from the wall, and the boys pulled Robert out to the ground. They panicked and thought he was dead at first. Robert was definitely out cold, and his head was bleeding. They called 911 and his parents and waited for help. The police arrived first and called for an ambulance to take him to the hospital.

Robert awoke in the hospital. At first, he couldn't remember what had happened. He quickly realized where he was and had a bad headache. He looked around the room and saw flowers, cards, and Get Well Soon balloons. He felt a bandage around his head. A nurse came in moments later and began talking to him.

"Oh, you're awake! My name's Sharon, and I've been taking care of you today. The doctors expected you to wake up at any time. I'll have to go let them know you're back with us. Your mom and grandma just left to get something to eat and should be right back."

"Nice to meet you, Sharon," Robert said. Then he croaked out, "How long have I been here?"

"You've been with us for four days."

"Holy shit! No way! Man, my head really hurts!"

"I don't know if you remember, but you were in a car wreck and hit your head," she said. "In a moment, I'll go let the doctor know you're awake, and then I'll give you something for the pain. You're very lucky; it could have been much worse."

Robert looked around the room again. To his right, he saw an old bald gentleman in an open gown shuffle in. Maybe the guy had dementia and had wandered in by accident. Robert was puzzled because the old guy seemed slightly transparent.

Robert unfortunately caught a glimpse of his old wrinkled, flabby ass and thought, *Oh shit! I can't unsee that!*

Embarrassed, Robert looked away, and when he looked back at him, the man was seated in a chair. The old man sighed and smacked his lips and breathed in deeply.

Smack, smack, suck.

The dry suction sound set Robert's teeth on edge. He began to wonder whether this was a deceased man. He seemed much more solid than what Robert had experienced in the past. He tried not to cringe. He didn't want to embarrass the man if he was in fact alive. But the continued smacking and sucking noises bothered him.

As Robert watched the man, he man began looking around the room as if he'd heard something. Robert thought the man seemed to turn his gaze at him for a moment.

"Uh, Sharon," Robert said.

"Yes, dear."

Robert pointed at the chair. "Is he supposed to be in here?"

The nurse glanced over. Her brow furrowed. "Who?"

Smack, suck, smack, suck.

"The old man," Robert replied.

She looked around the room and then back at Robert.

After a moment, she shook her head. "I don't see anyone. I'd better get the doctor. You just lie back. Try to get some rest."

Rest? Seriously?

Before Robert could stop her, the nurse left the room. She did that half-walk, half-run thing a person did when they wanted to hurry but didn't want to appear in a rush.

OK, so great—just him and the old man.

Smack, smack, suck, smack, suck.

At that moment, Robert's mom and grandma appeared in the hallway just outside the room, where Nurse Sharon told them he was finally awake and that she would be right back. As they entered the room and approached Robert's bed, Grandma momentarily directed her gaze at the old gentleman before her eyes settled on Robert.

"Are you doing OK?" she asked.

"So do you see the old man sitting over there?" Robert asked.

"What old man?" Robert's mom said.

Smack, suck, smack, suck.

Grandma grabbed his mother's hand. "There's a spirit of an old man sitting over there."

"Do you hear him?" Robert asked. "That sound is driving me crazy"

"I don't hear him making any sounds," Grandma replied. "What sound is he making?"

"It sounds as though he's gasping for breath."

At that moment, a doctor appeared with the nurse and walked to the bed. Grandma looked at Robert, grabbed his leg to get his attention, and held her finger up to her mouth for him to keep silent. The doctor began checking him out. He used a flashlight to check his eyes and responses to his hand movements.

"Hello. I'm Dr. Surbhi Anand."

Smack, suck, smack, suck.

He checked Robert's bandage and then said, "So I understand you saw a man in the room that Nurse Sharon didn't see. Is he here now?"

Smack, suck, smack, suck.

Robert looked at his grandma and then at his mom, then at the old man still sitting in his chair, staring straight ahead.

"No, he isn't."

Smack, suck, smack, suck.

Grandma smiled. "I think he remembered someone from his last visit to the hospital and really didn't see anyone."

"Is that true, Robert?" Dr. Anand asked.

Robert paused for a moment and looked at the old man. "Yes, that's correct," he said. "I think I just imagined him."

"What did he look like when you saw him?" Dr. Anand asked.

Robert described how he looked—elderly man in a hospital gown.

"Do you still have a headache?"

Smack, suck, smack, suck.

"Yes, I still have it," Robert said, "and it's mostly on the left side, where the injury is."

"So on a scale of one to ten, ten being the worst," Dr. Anand said, "how bad is your headache?"

"I'd say it's about a seven."

"That's not too bad. This didn't require surgery, but you took a pretty bad hit on the side of your head. You have a concussion and a slight brain bleed."

The doctor instructed the nurse to give Robert some Extra Strength Tylenol. Then he turned to Robert. "You'll likely have a headache for a while, but the Tylenol should help. Let us know if it doesn't."

Smack, suck, smack, suck.

Dr. Anand told Robert to alert the nurse if the vision came back or if something else occurred. Then he and the nurse left the room.

Grandma and Mom both offered to share their Cokes with Robert. He tentatively took a couple of sips, and it tasted great. Grandma was just looking at him and began holding his hand. They both told him they loved him, and he told them he loved them too. He was conflicted about them leaving with the man remaining in the room.

Smack, suck, smack, suck.

"What can I do to make the man leave my room?" Robert asked Grandma.

"Nothing," she replied. "He'll eventually leave on his own. Just be patient."

"We're so glad you've finally come around!" his mom said. "First thing: no more riding with that Jimmy."

"No kidding!" he said, starting to remember what had happened. "Was anyone else hurt during the accident?"

"No," his mom said. "No one else was hurt seriously."

Smack, suck, smack, suck.

"It's a good thing your head is so hard," Grandma said, "or you could've been hurt worse."

They all laughed.

During the night, the man in Robert's room simply disappeared while Robert was sleeping.

Over the next couple of days, several of Robert's friends, including Jimmy, came in to see him, as well as one of his teachers. His dad and his sisters came in to visit too. He stayed in the hospital only two more days before he was released. He never saw the old man again.

It would be a few weeks before he recovered completely from the accident and was allowed to go back to school. In the meantime, a couple of his friends dropped off his schoolwork so he could try to keep up. His grandma tended to him a lot during that time.

The doctors felt that even though the left side of his brain had been impacted, there should be no long-term damage, and few side effects. Robert now believed the injury had released this gift he'd inherited. Later, Grandma asked him a few questions about the old man in his room and smiled at some of his answers.

She said when she was younger, in Kentucky, she'd seen people who others didn't see and they seemed see-through. She tended to repeat herself from time to time. She said she'd even known some of the people and known they were dead. She told Robert that it might go away when he healed or it might not.

"You should consider it a gift if it stays," she said.

CHAPTER 3

ROBERT'S GIFT

Robert had since done some research on how many people were "blessed" with paranormal gifts similar to his. The variety of experiences people had was amazing. It was difficult for people like Robert to get anyone without such gifts to believe they possessed those capabilities, or went through their unique experiences, and science seemed to disprove these gifts. Perhaps God didn't want everyone to believe in this, or maybe it was the devil. Many scientists didn't believe in God, so it was no surprise that they didn't believe in the paranormal. But Robert did, and he believed in God too.

He also discovered others who'd had new talents or abilities released after a brain injury, particularly to the left side of the head, where art, imagination, and creativity lay—whereas the right side conducted logical, rational, scientific thinking.

Jason Padgett and Derek Amato were examples of this. Jason Padgett was attacked outside a karaoke bar and received a severe brain injury. Shortly after, he was recognized as a mathematics genius, but he also developed OCD and PTSD from his injury.

Derek Amato shallow dove into a swimming pool and obtained

a serious concussion. Shortly after his diving accident, he became a musical savant and started touring the world as a composer and pianist without having taken a single music lesson. They were both diagnosed as having developed a form of *acquired savant syndrome.*

There were also examples of people with head injuries who became evil too. Head injuries were much more prevalent in serial killers than in the average person. Edmund Kemper, John Wayne Gacy, and Ed Gein had suffered brain injuries, from a fall, accident, or physical abuse. They unfortunately had very bad physical and sexual abuse experiences growing up, too, which was a catalyst for some of their behavior.

Robert believed that was what had happened to him also. The gift presented itself more frequently, and became more solid and detailed, after his brain injury, and then the video or virtual experiences started coming. One day, after he talked about seeing someone unusual, his grandma grabbed his head between her hands and stared into his eyes.

"Now I see it!" she said. "You are like me now." She nodded, smiled, and smooched him on the lips, which she never did.

At the time, he didn't know what she meant. They continued to spend time together, and she told him more stories about her gift and, more importantly, how she responded.

"There are very few people who can see things like this, and you need to use it to help people. Promise me!"

"I promise!"

His poor grandma died a few months after that, from a stroke. She had always eaten badly. They were all very hurt that they'd lost her. Robert missed being able to talk to her. He wondered whether she'd become content when she thought she'd passed the gift along to him.

Robert had listened to everything she'd said throughout his life, even though he'd felt that some of her stories were just stories and imagination. He supposed that was from all the conditioning from his dad, friends, and schoolteachers he received growing up that suggested the paranormal could not exist. He'd read once that small kids were sponges for knowledge and beliefs and as they grew older were conditioned out of a lot. Even left-handed kids had once been told they shouldn't write or draw left-handed—they needed to work on using the right hand.

Robert did remember how Grandma had seemed to handle the occurrences, which she commented about occasionally and explained how people seemed to react with a smile, like she wasn't playing with all her faculties. She'd felt blessed to have her gift.

Robert's mom said that she'd talked to Grandma about his vision of the old man in the hospital room and that Grandma had explained that he was more gifted now after the accident and more gifted than she was.

Robert's family had to drive to Williamsburg, Kentucky, a couple of years after Grandma passed. It was on a cold, rainy day—the day of his aunt Dorothy's funeral.

A group of their family gathered in Williamsburg for his aunt's funeral service. Robert went inside with his family and walked around with his sisters, being approached by a number of people. Some of them he remembered, and some of them he didn't.

When he finally approached his aunt Dorothy's casket, he looked down at her and felt she was at peace now. Then something compelled him to touch her thin, wrinkled forearm skin. He was suddenly overtaken by a powerful vision of his aunt's hospital room. He could smell the antiseptic, alcohol smell of the facility and hear the constant beeping of the heart monitor. He could see his aunt lying in bed. He could tell she was barely alive, calmly looking around the room. She looked so frail and small.

Suddenly Aunt Dorothy rubbed her arms and said, "I'm so cold!" His aunt seemed to begin looking around the room as if she'd heard something. She gazed off in the distance and nodded a couple of times.

In a very weak and strained voice she faintly said, "Hello Bob. I love you too. Here I come, Mommy and Bobby."

Bobby was her husband, who'd passed a few years before. She closed her eyes, smiled really big, and just relaxed. The heart monitor stopped beeping and then droned a constant tone. As the nurse began walking toward her bed, Robert suddenly came out of the vision and back to reality, where his sister Tammy was talking to him and gently pulling him away from the casket.

"You had a vision, didn't you?" she said. "I could tell."

"Yes, I did."

"I saw something too!"

That was a big surprise to him. "We need to talk about that later, OK?"

"Sure," she said. "I'd love to talk about it."

Now Robert knew that his gift wasn't just tied to a place—it was also tied to a person. So being close to a body would also initiate a vision. Robert had a lot to reflect on during the drive home. When they were home later, Robert told his mom that he'd touched Aunt Dorothy and gone to her hospital room, and his mom just gazed at him, waiting for him to finish.

"Aunt Dorothy was happy," Robert said, "and seemed to be talking to Uncle Bob just before she passed away."

His mom said she was happy he had seen that and shared it with her.

During the time he was doing his research on the paranormal he also found historical information about when people had been interested in the paranormal. The earliest big following he found was the Spiritualist movement, which occurred from the 1840s to the 1920s. About eight million people worldwide followed this movement at its peak. It was a social religious movement that encompassed belief in the possibility of communication between the living and the deceased. It revolved around mediums such as the Fox sisters and Cora Scott and many times spirit guides conducting seances to communicate with the dead and ask for guidance.

Sir Arthur Conan Doyle and Charles Dickens were among members of the Ghost Club, which was founded in the mid-1800s to investigate ghosts and hauntings and still existed in the present day.

The paranormal also drew a lot of interest in the 1930s due to Frankenstein, Wolf Man, Dracula, and mummy movies. Boris Karloff, Lon Chaney, and Bela Lugosi were amazing! Robert read that Mr. Lugosi had been typecast in that role. He'd tried to break out into other roles, but it didn't go well. He'd actually been buried in his classic Dracula outfit.

In the 1970s, it once again became more popular. There had been a lot of interest in Ed and Lorraine Warren and their legacy. They'd actually performed thousands of paranormal investigations. The Enfield haunting that began in 1977 was confirmed by more than thirty people, including local police, firefighters, and news reporters. Robert loved these movies now and would have loved to have met the Warrens. Their investigations had been made into some very popular movies, beginning with *The Amityville Horror* and including *The Haunting in Connecticut*, *The Conjuring*, and *Annabelle*.

Lately there had been a wave of popular TV shows about ghost hunting in old schools, prisons, hospitals, churches, homes, nightclubs, and theaters around the world. There had even been shows about finding bigfoot and UFOs. Mankind had a fascination with the paranormal. The Catholic Church still had occasional group sessions to train clergy how to perform exorcisms.

CHAPTER 4

ROBERT'S ADULT LIFE

LIKE MOST MEN, ROBERT FELT HE NEEDED TO HAVE A GOOD JOB, A nice house, and a loving woman for him to be successful in life. So far, he hadn't figured out how to take advantage of his one true strength, his gift, to accomplish any of this. He couldn't get a house without a decent job, and he hadn't had much luck with women because his gift frightened them.

He decided to keep a standing ad in the *Cincinnati Enquirer* that had afforded him some money. He crafted the ad so that it wouldn't identify him. That plus miscellaneous jobs helped him pay his basic expenses of gas, apartment rent, and spending money.

He did have some interesting meetings and conversations from the ad and a few jobs. People asked him to join their paranormal groups or just asked him whether certain sites might be haunted. He did know that Cincinnati and Northern Kentucky had many haunted locations where a large number of people had experiences, such as Cincinnati's Music Hall and Washington Park, places beneath which a large number of corpses were still buried from the decades during which those locations were a potter's field and a civil war military hospital and cemetery, as well as the Sedamsville Rectory and Bobby Mackey's.

As an adult, after his gift vastly increased, Robert tried to avoid known haunted locations, including hospitals and cemeteries, since he could be flooded with visions. While he enjoyed watching crime TV shows and fictional murder mysteries, he avoided reading the newspaper, watching the TV news, or looking up recent crimes on the internet in case he was asked to visit a death scene although that had never happened yet.

He tried to date a few girls too, but nothing too serious. Two women he dated were Sandy and Teresa.

Robert was about six feet tall and 180 pounds. He had brown hair and a beard. His eyes were gray like his dad's. He had darker skin that tanned easily and wasn't unattractive.

He met Sandy at a party, and when she was introduced to him, she told him she'd heard he had paranormal gifts. Sandy thought it was very cool to know someone who saw things. She was pretty and very sexually active.

He began to feel like he could be more forthcoming with her until one night when they were at an Italian restaurant having dinner. He told her about a senior ghost couple who came into the restaurant and sat at a table close by. He told her they would stare at each other and smile, hold hands, and talk. Robert could faintly hear them talking. The waitstaff clearly avoided that table.

Robert asked a server, "Why don't you seat anyone at that table?"

"That's the table that Mr. and Mrs. Salvador sat at every Friday night for about twenty years, and we keep that table for them still every Friday night out of respect for them. They passed away close together about three years ago."

Robert quietly told Sandy what he saw, and at first, she acted like she was happy about the idea. Then she started pulling him a little closer and her smile was fading. She continued to ask him if they were still here and he admitted they were. He thought later that they should have left earlier, but they'd stayed too long. She seemed to be deep in thought the rest of the evening. She didn't want to stay with him that night. She suddenly began having other things to do when he tried to get together with her. The last he'd heard, she'd moved across the country to Seattle, Washington—a long drive from Ohio.

A short while after Sandy, Robert became interested in Teresa. They dated for a while, and their time together began without him telling her anything about his gift. He explained that he hadn't found a purpose in his life yet. She was a very pretty woman, with black hair and a medium complexion, and she was nicely built and wore dresses a lot, which was great! He was about twenty-four when they met.

They had a good time together. They spent a lot of time sitting around his or her apartment and ate popcorn and watched movies. He felt that not going out in public as often might help them, since he wouldn't be exposed to the deceased as much. They joked around a lot, and things were getting more serious. He had taken his time, and eventually they began making love, which was amazing. They had many things in common, and he hadn't been having many experiences lately.

She went to his family's house and met his parents and sisters, whom he had asked not to disclose his paranormal gifts. His mom and sisters adored Teresa, and Teresa seemed to enjoy that day too. They grilled out played cornhole and had a pleasant visit.

His mom pulled him aside. "How are things going with Teresa?"

"I'm still trying to figure out what to do about that," Robert replied.

"Well, maybe Teresa can help you figure things out."

"She doesn't know *anything* about my gifts yet."

They dated for about six months before things fell apart.

One Saturday, they went to visit her mom, Julie, for the day and hung out until after dinner. Julie lived just south of Hamilton, Ohio, an area that wasn't far from where Robert grew up, but Robert knew very little about. He thought he'd made a good impression with her mother that day. When they started to leave, Robert noticed a house two doors down. The house seemed to draw him, and he tried to avoid it to keep things normal, but he couldn't keep his eyes away.

Julie noticed him staring. "Oh, you're looking at the *murder house*."

"Oh no," Robert said. "That sounds bad. Why do they call it that?"

"That's such an awful story!" Julie said. "You haven't heard about it?"

"No, I haven't."

"On Easter Sunday in 1975, a very troubled man lost his mind and killed eleven of his family members there. After he killed them, he sat there for a while and then called the police and waited for them to come. He will spend the rest of his life in a mental health facility."

"Do you know if anyone else has seen anything unusual around the house?" Robert asked.

"I know the family that lives there," Julie said, "and they say they haven't seen or heard anything. In fact, what they complain about is people stopping by who want to enter the house to see if they can see or sense anything. They just want to be left alone."

There was nothing he could do. The murders were definitely drawing him in. When he came out of his gift, he was standing on the sidewalk by the house. Both Teresa and Julie were talking to him, and Teresa was even tugging his arm. They were asking him what was going on. After they said goodbye to Julie, the couple began the drive back to Teresa's apartment and were silent for nearly the whole ride.

Suddenly Teresa asked, "So have you seen other paranormal things in the past?"

"I don't know what you're talking about," Robert replied.

"I know you saw something because you were so focused. You couldn't even hear us talking to you! I've noticed you at other times in the past being distracted like that when I've been trying to talk to you. I did wonder where you were or what was going on."

When they arrived at her apartment, Teresa said, "You know, I think I'm just going to hang out by myself tonight and go to bed early."

She got out and walked away without the usual kiss.

The next day, Robert called her cell phone numerous times before she finally answered. When she finally picked up, he tried to act calm.

"Hey, how's it going?" he said. "I've been trying to reach you because last night was kind of odd, and please, I want to forget about it and move past this."

"Please don't lie to me. Are you a medium or a sensitive? Do you see things that others don't see?"

He was quiet for a moment. "Yes, I am. I inherited it from my grandma."

"So you can actually see ghosts?"

"Yes. Teresa, please—I care about you a lot, and it hasn't been a problem except yesterday. You are good for me, and I believe being with you helps keep these visions at bay."

She remained quiet for a while and then said, "I care about you too, but I need to think about whether I want to be part of that or not." She did not.

He had done something like this several times in the past and he would document what he saw at any visit he made, he started putting together a sort of portfolio of each experience. *Portfolio*—he hated that word for this. *Death journal* didn't sound very compassionate, but that's what he was doing by detailing each death experience from beginning to end.

It took Robert a few deaths when he first started this to figure out how to record each event. His first attempts weren't very good. So far, the people who had hired him had been satisfied with his death journal. *Satisfied* wasn't a great word either, but he couldn't say they were *happy.*

His latest death journal was about an ill elderly man, Mr. Henry Wilson, who'd lived north of Cincinnati and passed away alone. Mr. Wilson's family had found out about Robert and asked him to somehow capture Henry's death for them. He explained to them about how he documented everything he saw during his vision. He would write a detailed summary of everything step-by-step, describing the rooms, as well as the clothing anyone present wore, and even draw pictures of the rooms and people as he felt was necessary to share with family members for confirmation.

"We're very glad you can do that for us," they told him.

Two days later, Robert went to Mr. Wilson's house and found the key someone had left for him. When he entered, he believed the house was the same as it had been since Mr. Wilson had passed—minus his body, of course. Mr. Wilson hadn't been deceased long. Robert entered the home and walked around for a bit before he began feeling anything. He didn't notice any happy feelings, just a feeling of despair and loneliness. He noticed chemical odors probably from some cleaning that had occurred after Mr. Wilson passed and an underlying funky smell.

When he slipped into his vision, he saw a man who appeared to be in his late eighties or early nineties. Mr. Wilson was in his recliner in his living room wearing a housecoat. There was an IV on a portable stand in front of him. He was watching late-night TV with Jimmy Fallon and coughing as he laughed. He had a beer on the table he was drinking.

Robert had a strong feeling Mr. Wilson probably shouldn't have been drinking beer with the medication he would have been taking. Robert also saw an ashtray on the table filled with cigarette butts, so the man had obviously been smoking too. Robert found out later that Mr. Wilson had stopped taking his medication a few days before. He'd been ready to go and join his wife.

Mr. Wilson stood and held on to the wheeled IV pole and slowly hobbled to the bathroom to pee. Afterward, he hobbled back to his chair and sat down. He sat there watching TV for a few more minutes, laughing, coughing, and drinking his beer, and suddenly began a coughing spell, grabbed his chest with his left hand. "Oh shit!" he said. He held his left hand there and then held out his right hand as if he were reaching for something and his hands began shaking like he was trying to shake something off. He stopped and dropped his right hand in his lap, and then he closed his eyes and coughed a couple of times before his head fell forward and he passed.

Robert couldn't say Mr. Wilson was happy sitting there by himself, but he couldn't say he was sad either; this was normal for him. Robert of course had no idea what had been going through Mr. Wilson's head. The pain hadn't seemed severe by the way he acted, but Robert tried not to form his own conclusions. The man had had what appeared to be a heart attack, and then he passed. Right after he passed, Robert's vision ended, and he returned to the present time.

He wrote up his death journal for Mr. Wilson's family, and they were of course sad he had passed, but they'd already known that, of course. They were happy it hadn't been a terrible experience for him. Two of the women hugged Robert and cried. The rest shook his hand. They wished they could have been there for him, but it wasn't possible. They had moved away years ago. Robert could tell they didn't have much money, and he gladly accepted what they paid him.

Then there was his first murder vision. This one he would always remember because of the child. Robert was at home watching TV when the news broke in on the show he was watching. It was about a missing nine-year-old boy. The disappearance had just occurred very close to Robert's apartment. He suddenly had a feeling he could help. He drove to the crime scene right away and never had a clue about what really happened to the boy. He found out that the nine-year-old boy had simply gone missing.

The area hadn't been locked down yet since they were still gathering evidence. There were a couple of local news reporters on the scene to find out what they could. The police were talking to all the neighbors and taking down names. They had no idea where the boy was or what had happened to him yet. Robert slowly walked around the scene, and suddenly he saw a man staring at him. The man seemed to recognize something about Robert, as he appeared somewhat puzzled at first and then he panicked and ran into a garage and then into the adjoining house. Robert followed, and when he walked into the open garage, he stepped into his gift, or vision, and saw the entire scene. It was awful. It had all started here.

The neighbor had invited the boy into his garage to get a soda, and they talked and joked for a few minutes. The neighbor asked whether the boy would like to go into his house and get some cookies and watch TV or play video games. The boy must have felt something was wrong, and he said that he needed to leave because his parents didn't know where he was. The neighbor reached for the garage door button, and the garage door began closing.

The boy realized the neighbor didn't want him to leave and ran for the door. The door closed before he could reach it, and the boy began yelling and banging on the door with his fists. The neighbor walked over and grabbed the boy and put his hand over the boy's mouth to quiet him. He dragged the boy into the house, where he quickly taped his hands and mouth. Shortly after that, the neighbor began beating the boy, and once the boy was almost unconscious, he removed the boy's clothes and began touching him. Then he moved on to raping and sodomizing him.

Robert was horrified by the scene and knew this man needed to be prosecuted for his actions. He wished he could tune out the parts he didn't want to see. But he saw it all. Thankfully his visions processed faster than the real event—it sort of downloaded to him. It was as though the entire horrific event appeared in his mind in a few moments. He didn't understand how any of this happened. If this event took Robert as long to see as it took for it to occur, Robert would likely be a victim of this man, too, since he was in the vision and the present reality was gone.

He could sense the killer neighbor had done it before to other boys. His mistake this time was that he had picked a neighbor. How could anyone do this to anyone else, let alone a child? Eventually, when the pedophile neighbor was finished, Robert watched him wrap the boy in a rug and load him into the trunk of his car and drive away.

Robert's vision showed the man park close to the Great Miami River, get out, and walk around to make sure no one was nearby to witness his actions. He then carried the boy's body to a bush by the river and stuff it under the bush. Robert wondered why the neighbor hadn't thrown the boy in the river. The boy must have still been alive, because Robert's vision didn't end until the neighbor began to drive away. He didn't know the river very well, but Robert looked around for landmarks he could tell the police about.

Robert came out of his vision, quickly left the killer's garage, and approached a police detective who seemed in charge and began explaining his vision.

The cop waved his hand. "We're very busy here trying to find this boy. Please don't interfere with our investigation."

"Listen—I know what happened, and I know where the boy's body is."

The police officer stared at him, he put his hand on his pistol handle, and began to ask him some basic information, including how he'd come by the information.

Robert paused for a moment. "You won't believe me. Do you want to solve it or not?"

He knew they were under a lot of pressure to solve it right away.

"What's your name again?"

"Robert Anderson."

"Stay right here. I'm going to make a couple of phone calls." The officer stepped away and pulled out his cell phone.

After a few minutes, the officer put his phone away and said to Robert, "There are apparently a few officers who are aware of you and your *abilities*."

Robert knew the police had to do their due diligence, handcuffing him and taking him into custody first, but he was willing to take that chance. This man had to have some evidence in his house to confirm the awful event. The detective called another officer over to help take notes of Roberts story. The detective stared deep into Roberts eyes to try and see any tells that he may be lying.

Robert described what he'd seen in his vision—explaining that the neighbor had tricked the boy into his garage and then tried to get him into his house. The boy became anxious about the situation. The neighbor captured the poor boy, and Robert became visibly shaken as he explained what the neighbor had done to him, and that he'd eventually taken him to the riverbank in the trunk of his car.

"You really need to check into this perv," Robert added. "I think—no, I *know*—he has done this before, but not here."

He described some landmarks that made it easier for the police to narrow the search for the child. The police approached the house as the neighbor tried to escape out his back door. The police arrested him and put him in handcuffs, hauled him out front, and placed him in the back seat of a police car. The pedophile was crying now. The other neighbors started gathering around them, listening. It was a blessing that the boy's parents were in their house with other police officers. Based on the description Robert gave, they quickly located the body.

One of the neighbors was a big man, and he said, "You know, I knew this guy was trouble!" glaring at the pedophile the whole time. "Why don't you let him out of the car for a few minutes? I'd like to talk to him! I'd like to make him bleed."

Robert had to go to the police station and fill out a police report on what he'd experienced before they released him. He met the boys poor parents briefly and told them how sorry he was for what that man did. The police gave him veiled recognition, but that was OK. They didn't know how to explain witness testimony like this. Robert had helped solve the crime for the family. It was something that may have taken weeks or months to solve otherwise. The police took the credit. Robert was considered a witness. Mainly, this was one more sick fuck was off the street!

CHAPTER 5
FIRST DEATH JOURNAL

AFTER THE DAY AT THE OLD HOUSE AND THE ATTACK ROBERT witnessed, he stayed in his hotel room by himself, ordered room service, and filled his *death journal* with details about the murder he'd witnessed. He usually didn't forget details in assembling things like this. Robert had also not long ago taken some art classes in college that helped with his drawings.

He believed the first murder had happened about three or four years ago. There was something about the police investigation and their conclusion that the group of surviving family members didn't believe. They'd paid the private investigator to obtain copies of the police reports of all the murders. While the police were satisfied that the case was closed with the man who'd killed himself, the families weren't quite so sure and wanted Robert's expertise to see what he could find out.

The day he had receive the call was a nice day outside, sunny yet cool, just like today. He had just gotten back from a run around the Lunken airport track.

Mr. White told him to be prepared to stay two or three weeks. Robert had no idea how many clothes to take for that much time.

He sat in the hotel room, pulled out a new blank notebook, and began documenting the horrible experience from the beginning to the end. He didn't leave out any details regarding what he'd seen. He would describe the exterior and appearance of the house and yard. He recorded the visit from when he arrived to when he left the place.

Robert detailed the spot in the house where he believed the vagrant had lived and how he'd put himself into the vision and what that felt like. He documented the actual crime in depth. Robert really tried not to offer his opinion on any of this, but sometimes he mistakenly put it in. He drew pictures of the house and some of the details in rooms to demonstrate where things physically occurred.

He sketched the victim and the killer, in this case to both demonstrate their difference in size and capture their faces. He produced a couple of figure drawings to show where they were positioned. On the way to share his experience with the family, he stopped by the library and made copies of his journal and stapled the sheets together.

When he arrived, he saw that the Whites had a nice house. It was in an upper-class neighborhood—Robert had learned Mr. White was an executive at a large company, about to retire—and he had to park down the street a little bit. Robert had the address, so it was easy to find, plus there were several cars and trucks around the house. It was a large brick two-story. The furniture was very nice too. They had a beautiful grandfather clock clicking away the whole time. There were several people in the room murmuring as they discussed whatever they were talking about.

They had someone serving drinks and snacks before the meeting started. Robert took a water to soothe his throat while he talked. Mrs. White stayed next to her husband Mr. White, holding his arm. The victim had looked a lot like her mother. Mr. White looked as though he might be ill, but anyone who had to go through something like this might seem that way and certainly wouldn't be happy or outgoing. This would take a toll on anyone.

Robert walked into the room, and a hush came over the gathering for a few moments—and then the murmuring began again. Robert walked over to Mr. White and introduced himself. Mr. White had seen a picture of Robert, so he knew who he was. Robert felt really bad for Mr. White and his wife.

"I'm so sorry for your loss," Robert said shook hands with the Whites.

It was tragic that they'd finally gotten to the point where they could relax and retire and they lost someone so close to them. Mrs. White said they had other grown children, so they still had family to share their lives with, but losing a child was one of the most difficult things a parent could go through. Robert hoped he never had to experience it.

Mr. White began the evening politely but directly.

"Please, everyone, take a seat so that we can get started. Please be quiet throughout this process. Please call me Samuel, and this is Robert Anderson. As you all probably know, except for Robert, the last time our daughter Carolyn was seen alive was right after she got off work the day she disappeared.

"She was working at a retail store, saving money for college, even though she didn't need to, and for the experience. She walked to a Starbucks and got a coffee and went into the small parking lot that was behind the strip mall where she worked and apparently unlocked her car and put her purse and phone in it and then disappeared.

"One of the other employees, who was a friend, came out a few minutes later and noticed that Carolyn's car was still parked there. Her coffee was dropped outside the driver's door, and he noticed that her purse and phone were in it and it was unlocked. Her friend thought that very odd, so he waited a few minutes, watching the car, and, when she didn't return, called the police, who arrived about ten minutes later. It went downhill from there, and she was discovered by the police in the house we sent Robert to."

Robert handed out the copies of the journals he'd made right before they started.

"I don't need to know everyone's names," Robert said, "because I won't remember them. I have always been bad remembering names."

He began to tell them about himself and his experiences, but before he could share what he usually said about himself, Mr. White stopped him and asked him to get to his experiences from the journal.

"I'm sorry to stop you, but we already know about your skills," Mr. White said, "and that's why we hired you."

The private investigator they hired to find Robert couldn't make it today but would likely be at the next meeting.

You could tell Mr. White was accustomed to leading meetings like this. He seemed a little blunt in how he'd addressed him, but Robert didn't mind.

"At the beginning of movies," Robert said, "they make a disclaimer if a movie is not appropriate for everyone. I assure you my *death journals* and what I'm about to share are not appropriate for everyone, as you will see. If you get too upset, you may want to step out of the room. I leave out no details as I see them. Anything may be a clue."

He asked them to hold their questions until the end and said he'd answer everything.

The White family and a few other adults were present when Robert began to tell them what he'd witnessed. He assumed the others were from a couple of families who had also lost someone because of this madman. He more or less read the details that he'd documented in his journal.

He explained how he'd felt as he approached the house the first time and why he stopped and returned for the second visit. Robert went step-by-step through the experience, from the beginning to the end, in graphic detail.

He stopped a couple of times when he saw someone get very upset. Two of the women were crying, and everyone else was silent. Mrs. White was also crying. Three people left the room during his account of what happened to the beautiful young woman. Most of them flipped through the handout as he read and explained it. Some of them were taking notes.

Once he finished telling them what he'd witnessed and documented, Mr. White read some of the details of the police report, which seemed to match well with the vision Robert journaled. Mr. White then pulled out a picture of their daughter Carolyn, who was lovely and looked exactly like the woman Robert witnessed being murdered. He reminded them the killer had taken their daughter's St. Christopher's pendent, too, as a trophy.

Then Mr. White produced a picture of the presumed killer and held up the picture of the man Robert had drawn, which was received with a series of comments such as "We knew it!" and "Oh my God." The picture of the police suspect wasn't close to the vision of the man Robert had seen with the knife. There was no mistake—it wasn't him.

They seemed justified now that the man Robert had seen was different from the man the police blamed. So the man they believed killed the young women was probably innocent of these crimes, which meant the killer was still out there. The police had stopped trying to solve the case because they thought they already had. The case had been closed.

"I know the police are under a great deal of pressure to resolve any serious cases like this," Robert said, "and their suspect for some reason seemed like a good fit to them. There are many examples where someone innocent is convicted of murders they didn't commit in the police's efforts to resolve the case and make others feel comfortable."

He knew the families were going to reach out to the police, so he would be talking to them and receiving their scrutiny and skepticism soon. Hopefully they would still try to ID the drawing he'd made.

At that moment, Robert decided he also wanted to visit the location where the suspected killer had died too. He needed to determine if the innocent man was killed by the man he'd seen or if he'd killed himself. There were some very good questions from several of the people. Robert took some notes, too, for the next visit.

At the end of the Whites' family meeting, Mr. White asked Robert whether he was comfortable where he was staying and whether he needed anything. Robert told him he would need a day to relax before he went to the next house. Mr. White said he was fine with that.

Mrs. White grabbed Robert's hand. "Thank you so much for helping us," she said and smiled as tears ran down her face.

Mr. White gave Robert an envelope with more cash in it for his expenses, and he and his wife thanked Robert. Then most of the people came over to shake Robert's hand and thank him. Some of the people stared at him like maybe they were trying to see something, which he was used to. Mr. White finally gave Robert an envelope containing the location of the second house and where the young woman had been killed inside it, according to the police. Robert didn't open the envelope yet—he wanted to wait until later.

CHAPTER 6

DETOX AND SECOND DEATH HOUSE

ROBERT HAD WORKED ONLY A COUPLE OF BAD CASES LIKE THIS BEFORE he'd decided he needed to spend some time relaxing and unwinding before visiting the next location. He referred to this as his 'detox' time. On this occasion, he first went outside and took a short walk to loosen up. It was nice weather—neither too hot nor too cool. Then, to refresh his mind, he went to the hotel bar to settle in and do some brainless things to forget about what had happened. He enjoyed watching football and soccer games.

I should try to learn yoga or meditate to do a better job of relaxing instead of watching junk TV and drinking bourbon, he thought. He also remembered that he needed to check with his sister Tammy to see whether she'd go with him on one of these types of visits to see whether she could sense anything and keep him company.

Two days after he shared his death journal with the families, Robert felt recovered enough from visiting the first house and discussing his experience with the families. Visiting murder scenes was certainly much more traumatic than witnessing end-of-life death scenes. He woke fairly early and got ready to go to the second murder house. It was once again a nice, sunny fall day. He had some breakfast and drank some coffee at the hotel before he left for the second house, which was about thirty miles southwest of the first. It was a newer house in a nicer neighborhood, and people lived there, but they'd been asked not to be home that day.

It was around noon when Robert arrived at this house. There was a police car outside the home—keeping an eye on him, he supposed. After Robert got out of his car and headed toward the door of the home, a police sergeant got out of the car and approached him.

"Are you Robert Anderson?"

"Yes, sir, I am."

"My chief sent me to tell you that you're not going to find anything in any of these houses with your magic wand other than what we found. I don't feel like I need to tell you this, but we did a thorough job investigating these houses, and I hope you know the killer was identified and is deceased and the cases are now closed."

"If I don't find anything different from what you found," Robert said, "at least the families will know and be satisfied. I hope you're right and that the killer is actually dead."

"Don't stay in there too long, because I have actual police work to do."

"I don't know how long it will take," Robert said, "but I'll try to hurry the magic up."

The sergeant stared Robert down for a few moments more, trying to intimidate him, as Robert returned his gaze with a smile. Then he shook his head and returned to his car and Robert entered the house.

Robert's visit began with his looking at the furniture and wall hangings and noticing the cleanliness of the space as he walked from room to room for about an hour, during which nothing happened. The place was tidy. He did hear the light family history of laughter and activity, like he usually did.

Robert wasn't sure where this death lay in the order of the several deaths since he insisted on not knowing anything. He did, however, ask for the location of the death within the house. Knowing the area in which the crime occurred helped him narrow things down a little. Of course, where the crime scene investigators believed it occurred might not be precise, but it usually was. All the evidence, of course, had been cleaned up and removed too. Later he heard they'd had a difficult time selling the house because of the murder, but it was a newer, attractive home, and eventually they'd found this family, who got a very good deal on it.

Later Robert was told the family that lived there now had lived here for a couple of years and hadn't experienced anything, which was normal, since it took a certain sensitivity to experience most things like this.

He was very glad most people normally couldn't see or sense these disturbing things. There were a lot of shows on TV that represented folks who saw ghosts and spirits, and he would never judge those shows or those people. Some of those places were haunted places where the deceased were cruel or evil in life and remained to continue to haunt and torture the people who tried to occupy the places where they'd expired.

Robert believed demons existed too, but thankfully, so far, he didn't feel as though he'd experienced any. It was extraordinary that there was such a wide variety of ways gifted people sensed things like this. Some people just got a bad feeling, while others smelled or heard things. Some people saw things but didn't hear things. Robert's gift caused him to experience more than most. He could smell the blood, or body odor, or bleach, and many other smells. He could hear the moans and laughter and screaming. He saw some good echoes from the past, but mainly he just heard them. He saw death. It was profound, and he was still trying to understand it. He hoped his grandma had never experienced some of these things.

He decided it was time to leave and return the next day, as it sometimes took a couple of visits for him to immerse himself in bad events. As he was going out the door, he heard a loud bang and a moan. He slowly shut the door, and as he turned, he was immersed in the vision.

He now saw a totally different living room. All the furniture was different and rearranged in the space, and the walls were painted another color. So this was the room where the police thought it happened, and nothing seemed out of the ordinary yet. Then Robert heard noises from another room. He walked toward the next room, which he knew was the kitchen, and he detected the body odor smell he'd encountered at the first house. When he entered, he discovered a woman—an attractive redhead—nearly hidden by the large man. His back was to Robert, but Robert was sure it was the man from the first house.

The kitchen was rather large and had the same cabinets as in the present but with different appliances. There was a window over the sink looking into the backyard, and now the day, or that day, looked rainy and dark. On the far right of the room there was a door to the backyard standing slightly open, and he could hear the drizzle. The clock on the wall ticked loudly and showed it was about a quarter after two.

The pretty redheaded woman was in her apron with a knife in her hand, leaning back against the cabinet.

"Get out of my house!" she yelled. "Get out right now. What are you doing in my house? How did you get in here?"

He was in front of her, still looking disheveled as before, wearing the same clothes. Robert moved closer and saw the man grinning and laughing at her. He seemed to be as manic as the first time. He had those gloves on again to keep from leaving his fingerprints behind, though now any hair or blood trace evidence could potentially identify the killer through DNA.

The woman swiped the knife as the man reached out to her and quickly pulled back only to try it again. She was clearly terrified, crying and moaning. She swiped at him three or four times, and then he finally grabbed her wrist and pulled her to him. He tried to kiss her mouth, but she turned her head, and he laughed at her before kissing her cheek.

She put her right hand in his face and scratched his left cheek. He laughed and then growled. Robert needed to remember the scratches. The man didn't appear to be bothered too much by the cuts on his cheek. He squeezed her hand until she yelped, forcing her to drop the knife on the floor. He leaned forward and bit her neck pretty hard. She screamed and tried to pull back. He appeared to be trying to tear a piece of her neck off with his bite but failed. Robert was sure he was leaving DNA from his saliva on her neck.

The man finally grabbed her by the neck with his large hands and started squeezing it. She began striking him with the palms of both hands, trying to get free, fighting for her life. He was still choking her.

She coughed and moaned and then lowered her hands as she began passing out.

He released his grip and allowed her to recover. As she did, and started fighting again, he resumed chocking her. She coughed again, trying to catch her breath. He was playing with her. She kicked her feet up to try to protect herself. He shoved her back against the cabinets and pushed his body up against hers, between her legs. Robert could tell he was trying to rub his groin against hers.

"Please, sir—I have a child! Please don't kill her mother. Do what you want to me, but please don't kill me! I don't want to die! Where is your mother? I'm sure you wouldn't want her killed."

He paused for a moment and tilted his head, looking at her face, and gave her a wicked smile. Then he pulled a knife from the rear of his pants, and she was shocked on seeing it. He also had the sledgehammer lying on the island behind him, but he didn't use it.

"Mother?" the man said. "My mother never protected me. Bitch."

He gently, lightly slid the knife down her ear and throat. She stared at the knife, terrified. He cut her apron straps, then cut her blouse and bra open, exposing her breasts. She tried to pull her clothes back together. He grabbed one of her breasts with his left hand while holding the knife to her throat with his right. He squeezed her breast forcibly.

"Oh yes," he said, "very nice. You are very pretty!" He had a deep, growly, slurry voice. He continued squeezing.

Then the killer looked in her eyes and slid the knife slowly into her ribs. She looked down at the knife entering her body and screamed, using her fists to strike his face and shoulders. "No!"

He loved it and laughed harder and louder. He leaned his face close to hers and licked her cheek, like he had with the other woman. Once the knife was embedded in her, he slowly began pulling it out. Once he removed it, he brought it higher on her chest and slowly slid it back in again, just below her left breast. He was much closer to her heart. She moaned, and by the amount of blood that flowed out, Robert knew he had struck something important that time. He thought the man nicked or sliced one of the arteries feeding blood from her heart.

Her eyes became large as her face tightened and she groaned.

"No—please don't."

He slid it in up to the handle again and rotated the blade around. She leaned backward as he removed the knife from her chest. He then moved the knife to her throat and quickly sliced back and forth, much harder and deeper than with the first woman Robert had witnessed him kill. He then sliced her exposed torso from the neck slice to her mons pubis, which also began bleeding.

Her blood flowed and spurted down her neck and the front of her body. The slice went deeper this time, probably because he was at a better angle between her legs. Her head tipped back since the knife had gone so deep, probably cutting muscles too. Robert felt like he had sliced through her carotid artery and jugular vein. But she couldn't be dead yet, since Robert was still present.

Robert hoped she at least wasn't feeling pain at this point. He had always read that it was very difficult to cut someone's head off with a knife. For his own sake, Robert was glad the man wasn't successful. That would have been horrible to witness. She was such a beautiful woman and mother. He felt so sorry for the woman and now hated this man. Robert got a little sick to his stomach and almost threw up. He wanted to turn away, but he needed to catch every detail.

Her blood was flowing and spurting all around her, including on her murderer. The man then took the knife as before and dragged it down the center of her body from her neck to her groin. There wasn't much blood flowing out from this cut, so Robert figured her heart had nearly stopped.

Robert needed to remember more details about the man this time to better ID him. He walked up closer to them. He didn't know whether he could come back and see any vision a second time. He had yet to try that. The killer had dark hair on his forearms and a small tattoo on his left forearm that Robert recognized as a four-leaf clover with a dagger sticking through it.

"You pathetic son of a bitch," Robert said.

The killer was concentrating on what he was doing, but he quickly turned his head toward Robert and looked confused. He then smiled and laughed. Robert knew he sensed something!

The man picked her body up like she weighed nothing and carried her to the living room, where police thought most of the crime had taken place. Surprisingly, when Robert looked back, most of the victim's blood remained on her person. Robert followed the killer into the living room as he laid her on her back on the coffee table. He turned her head so that she was staring at the couch and pulled her hair back to expose her face.

He sat down and looked at what he had done. He moved her blouse so that her breasts were exposed. He reached out and touched each of her nipples with his gloved index finger. He then pulled his right glove off and touched each of her nipples with his bare hand and squeezed her breasts with his palm before putting the glove back on. He slid his hand inside her panties, touching her most private place, moving his hand around, and she never reacted

He slowly turned his head and stared in Robert's direction for a few moments, then nervously laughed. His smile faded briefly. Did he sense Robert?

He couldn't sense me, since I wasn't there at the time.

Robert didn't understand.

She suddenly moaned loudly and opened her eyes. The killer looked into her eyes. He began rubbing the front of his pants to try to satisfy himself while he stared at her, and then he moaned. He seemed much more comfortable this time. Of course, Robert had no idea what had happened before the crime scene unfolded. But he now understood how they thought the living room was the crime scene. There was so much blood here, even though her blood had stopped flowing.

There was a lot of blood on her clothes and running off her body. The man had her placed in a position that he was proud of, and Robert thought he was done. The killer reached and removed two ornate barrettes from her hair and put them in his pocket. Trophies. He also cut off some of her hair and took it, like he had with the other woman. He was developing a pattern. Who knew what compelled him to do what he did?

The killer went into the kitchen and returned with his hammer and two Budweisers from the refrigerator and sat down on the couch. He sat one beer on the table near the victim's face as he started drinking the other.

In a deep, slow, slurred voice, he said, "How has your day been so far, dear? Oh, I hope it gets better." He chuckled. "I don't think so, though. You have some nice tits there. I wish I had a camera."

He finished off the first beer, crushed the can in his hands, and put it in a pocket. Then he picked up the second beer.

"Well," he said, "I've got to go before your husband gets home. Won't he be surprised?"

He stood, sticking the unopened Budweiser and the hammer in a pocket, and walked toward the kitchen door. He turned around and looked back at the entire scene. He seemed to take pride in what he had done. He looked toward where Robert stood and paused for a moment.

Robert said, "I'm going to stop you and hopefully kill you, you fucker."

The man seemed to growl a little bit, and then he shook his head and opened the back door. It was still raining outside as he left.

Moments after that, the vision disappeared, and the normal living room came back to Robert, who staggered and almost fell down. Sometimes that happened when he left the vision—he believed he was switching from one reality to the other and his perception of gravity was not the same, or maybe it was from the trauma he'd experienced.

Once again, the furniture and its configuration reflected that of the new owners. The smell of the room returned to the clean normal smell too. He walked into the kitchen again to look around for any signs.

Robert decided it was time for him to leave also. He opened the door to the bright sunny day outside. The police car was gone. He guessed the sergeant had decided he needed to get back to work. Robert went out and got in his Jeep and jotted down a few notes.

"I've got to stop him somehow!"

He recorded some comments as reminders for his journal later. He had been in there for nearly an hour, including the time before the vision had kicked in. The weather was still pleasant, and it would be a nice drive back to the hotel, except the day was not the same for him any longer.

CHAPTER 7
THE SECOND DEATH JOURNAL

ROBERT SPENT THE NEXT TWO DAYS RECALLING, DOCUMENTING, AND reviewing in his death journal what he'd experienced. He drew and wrote everything he could to help. He wanted to ensure that he had all the details correct and that the police had nothing to doubt this time around. He wanted everyone to know that this woman had scratched the killer's face with her right hand, and that the killer had licked her left cheek and bit her neck.

Robert didn't know how long DNA like that would last under the victim's nails, but it was an important thing to detail. It took him an entire day to fill out this death journal, including the drawings. He contacted Mr. White that he was ready for the next family meeting, and they scheduled a time for the next day.

Robert got up the following morning, ate, and headed out for the Whites' house once again. He was on his way to meet with certain members of the White family, plus members of the second family, which turned out to be the McKensey family and Mr. Dorsey. He once again stopped at the library and made copies of his death journal. He always made a couple of extra copies to keep for himself too.

He noticed a library worker trying to see what he was copying on their copier, but he kept it secret. When he arrived at the Whites house several members of the McKensey and Dorsey family were there. Other people were there, too, probably from additional families who had lost a daughter or wife.

Like the first time, Robert went over and spoke to Mr. and Mrs. White first since they were the hosts and he knew them the best.

Mrs. White looked at him and said, “I don’t understand how you can do this. It has to be a horrible experience. We are of course very grateful.”

“Before my grandma passed away,” Robert said, “she knew I had this gift and made me promise that I would use it to help people, like she had done when she was younger. As the saying goes, it’s a blessing and a curse.”

He told Mr. White before they started about the police officer’s discussion with Robert, and he said that was not uncommon. Mr. White was dressed sharply but looked sad and run down. Mrs. White went to get Robert a drink while he handed out copies of his death journal to the family members. Mr. White stood and prepared to begin the meeting. There was again a range of emotions among those in the room, but once the meeting commenced, everyone was attentive to what he said and documented. There were about the same number of people that had been there the first time. Robert was relieved they hadn’t brought any children. Mr. White continued the meeting once again, which Robert liked.

“As you all know, this is about Mr. Anderson’s visit to witness the demise of the poor young woman who was a mother, a wife, and a daughter named Rose McKensey-Dorsey. Mr. Anderson, if you would be so kind as to begin telling us about this horrible event.”

As he had the first time, Robert said up front, “This is not going to be for everyone. Please leave the room if you get overwhelmed. As you all know, this is my death journal, which documents all my experiences at the location.”

He began reading his death journal to the group. He walked through the entire crime, and shortly into his describing the scene in the kitchen, a couple of women began crying, so they got up and left the room. Robert decided to play down certain details, such as the amount of blood he saw and the pleasure the killer obtained from this murder.

He didn't discuss the fact that the killer had masturbated through his pants as he looked at her body in the living room, even though that part was included in his journal. He made sure he brought up that the killer had taken Rose's hair barrettes, and he described them.

"I was with Rose when she bought them," Rose's mother said, "and they looked beautiful in her hair."

He learned that Rose McKensey-Dorsey was married and had a daughter. Her mother and father and siblings were in attendance. Robert also met her husband, who nodded and cried the entire time. He was a good-looking redheaded guy. That poor man would never be the same. Robert felt so bad for all her family, but especially for him. Robert didn't know who some of the other people were. You could tell Rose's family members because of the way they reacted—he didn't need his gift to be able to perceive that. He took some extra time to pay attention to her family, like he had the White family after the first meeting.

He learned the private investigator named Sheila Flores was here this time too. At the end, she came forward to introduce herself to him. He thought she was very attractive. He also noticed that she took a lot of notes about what he said and asked whether she could make copies of everything. He told her that it was up to the families, as it was their information now. Once Sheila Flores got involved, the police didn't bother him again.

Sheila admitted to Robert that she still wasn't entirely sure what to do with this information yet, and that she wasn't sure what to think of him, even. From the research she'd done on him, she said, he really seemed legitimate. Like most people Robert met, she'd never believed in this sort of paranormal ability before.

"Two of my police brothers laughed about engaging you," Sheila said, "but my brother Jason said I should give you a try. He heard your name from people he trusted and thought you might be the real thing. I certainly understand why the families have been interested in pursuing information beyond what the police have done. Sometimes the police look for a fast, easy solution."

"They're under a lot of pressure from the media and their chief to solve cases quickly, as you probably know.

"I'm not sure I believe Tim Higgins was the killer either. It doesn't make any sense—although he had been in locations close to a couple of the murders when they happened."

There was no physical evidence to link anyone to the murders, which happened sometimes. Serials wanted to kill. Serials usually did their very best to avoid being discovered. They wanted to continue on their mission of death because of whatever trigger started them.

"I haven't heard of very many serials who were drug addicts either," Sheila said.

The information she knew about Tim Higgins didn't quite fit. However, the murders had stopped after he died, which gave the police more validation about him.

Sheila told Robert that she felt he had withdrawn into himself, when he was explaining his experience as though he was reliving the entire thing.

She said, "I would love to get to know you better and try to understand what you are experiencing."

She said, "If this skill you have turns out to be the real thing, what a powerful tool you could be in helping stop these crimes and put these assholes away, where they belong." She thought she might call Mr. Anderson and take him out to eat to get to know him better.

Robert finished answering questions, trying to be sympathetic to the family. He was speaking to Mr. White when Mr. McKensey approached them with some awful information.

"I wanted you to know," Mr. McKensey said, "that that day, her husband, Mitch, was carrying their daughter in after picking her up from day care when he discovered Rose. He quickly went back out to his car and called the police and then us. He is devastated."

When Mitch joined the men, Robert reached out and shook his hand and almost wanted to hug him.

"I am so sorry for your loss," Robert said. "We'll get this son of a bitch. I promise you!"

Mitch nodded. "Thank you," he said weakly.

Mr. McKensey asked some more questions, and then they were

thanking Robert for sharing what had happened despite the horrible outcome.

Sheila said, "I did some research trying to find out how we might be able to figure this out and my brother Jason said he had a friend who was into the paranormal and thought this man from Cincinnati might be able to help us."

"I think I can. I've been doing this sort of thing for a while."

Mr. White said, "We believe you are exactly what we need to accomplish what we're trying to do, and we really appreciate it."

"The police usually don't believe this because they need facts," Robert said, "and let's face it—these aren't facts you can prove."

Sheila said, "I really want to get to know you better and what you can do, if you're amenable to that."

Robert smiled, "I'm fine with that. I have nothing to hide."

Once again, at the end of the family meeting, Mr. White gave Robert an envelope containing the location of the next house and where the third young woman had been killed inside, according to the police. He didn't look at that information yet.

He was detoxing again. He drove back to the hotel and was relaxing at the bar, drinking a decent Four Roses bourbon, befriending one of the bartenders, Landon, and watching soccer on the TV. He was playing games on his phone when suddenly it rang. It was Sheila Flores.

"How are you doing?" she asked.

"I'm doing better," Robert said, "but I need to get my mind off this for a bit before I immerse myself in it again."

"Would you like to go out to dinner? It would be my treat."

He stalled for a moment and thought about telling her no.

"I promise I won't talk about any of this if you don't want to."

"I would be glad to."

So they made plans for that evening to go out to eat. He finished his bourbon and realized he had an hour to get ready. He said goodbye to Landon and went to his room. He thought about taking a shower but didn't feel energetic enough to do it. He just relaxed on the bed with the TV on. He wondered how this dinner would go with a private investigator and whether she might have an ulterior motive. But she seemed like a nice person, so why not?

They went to a local steak house and had a nice steak dinner and a bottle of cabernet. Sheila was very pretty when she smiled.

She began making small talk with him, calling him "Mr. Anderson."

He laughed. "Please call me Robert or Rob. Calling me Mr. Anderson reminds me of *The Matrix*!"

They both laughed.

"That's fine," she said, "if you'll call me Sheila."

He agreed.

They talked to each other at length about themselves and their families.

"I grew up with my mother, father, and five brothers in Pittsburgh," Sheila said. "We had a great life. Dad was a cop most of his life but passed away of natural causes about five years ago.

"Three of my brothers, Michael, Frank, and Jason, became cops, too, to follow in our father's footsteps. Michael is actually a detective. As for my other two brothers, James works in IT and David is an accountant.

"I wanted to do something different and decided to go in the army for one tour, and when I got out, I decided to become a PI. I enjoy it and get to set my own hours and make decent money."

She seems pretty darn smart, Robert thought. *I have such a hard time with women because of my gift. Well, maybe it's not just my gift—maybe it's me too.*

Sheila asked a lot of questions about him, but he felt that he had nothing to hide and she was really nice, so he addressed everything she brought up. She asked all about his family and how he'd obtained his paranormal gift, so he explained the entire situation to her.

At the end of the evening, Sheila asked, "Do you mind if I go to the next location with you? And when do you think you'll be ready to go—tomorrow or the following day?"

He thought for a moment. "I have no problem with you going too. Actually, I think that would be a great idea. And I should be ready to go tomorrow, thanks to you."

He knew she wouldn't interfere with his vision since he went so deep now. She also asked him whether he'd mind if she brought a video camera too. He said it would be fine if she wanted to video record the incidents but that he'd tried it before and nothing paranormal showed on video.

"I thought about investing in some of the other paranormal equipment," Robert said, "like an EVP recorder, an EMF detector, et cetera, but I can't afford those things yet, and it would be nearly impossible to do those by myself.

"I also need to concentrate to be able to transition into my vision. I set up a video camera once on a tripod and wasn't able to capture anything paranormal on it."

This had been a great detox for him so far, talking to someone like this. He'd never had someone interested in finding out about him before in such a nice way. The two finished around eleven o'clock, and Sheila took Robert back to the hotel. As she was about to leave, she said, "OK. I'll pick you up in the morning around, say, nine?"

"Nine should be fine."

"I'll bring some doughnuts from my favorite shop, Peace Love & Little Donuts."

"That sounds good," Robert replied.

He wondered whether Sheila thought he was faking this and might catch him by being there herself. He was happy since he was by no means faking this.

CHAPTER 8
THIRD DEATH HOUSE

The next house, the third house, was currently vacant. Robert liked that better. The house was in a more urban area, which was different from the last two. They'd been in more rural locations, but so far, the homes weren't too far apart. This one was about forty-five miles from the last one and fifteen miles from the first one.

The morning after their dinner, Sheila picked Robert up with some great doughnuts and coffee, and they headed to the third location.

"I'm really nervous," Sheila said.

"I understand," Robert said. "You don't need to worry about anything—just relax. You probably won't experience anything, but you may be a little freaked when I go into my vision."

It had been three days since the last location. There was a police car outside again when they got out of Sheila's Buick. She waved at the officer, and he waved back. She had brought a video camera.

The lawn was well maintained. In the backyard was a swing set, and out front a small bicycle lay near a For Sale sign featuring a local real estate agent. So now Robert knew that a child or children had lived here. Kids living here made him happy but concerned.

To Robert, it seemed like any other normal brick ranch home on that block, until they passed the sidewalk into the yard. A ripple of his vision briefly hit him, and he paused for a second.

Sheila grabbed his arm when she saw him back up a little bit.

"I'm OK, thanks," he said, "but it's beginning."

He approached the front door with Sheila close behind. He stepped across the small front porch and touched the glass storm door. Nothing further happened when he opened it and took the door handle.

Once he opened the door and stepped inside, he saw no furniture—the place was clean—but the room began changing. There was a slight shimmer or vibration surrounding him as he entered the house.

"Here we go," he said.

He entered the gift vision at a shallow level. He suddenly sensed positive feelings all about him. He looked around and now saw simple clean furniture and clearly a minimalist sort of style. He saw a box with kids' toys stacked in it. He heard kids playing and a woman laughing—the joyful noise surrounding him, emanating from throughout the home. It made him smile.

The darkness wasn't coming through yet. He was still in a shallow, happy state, so he could still see Sheila. She, too, was looking around the space. Robert was pretty sure she didn't see or feel anything. He looked in the kitchen, and it was clean and simple too, with the countertops free of dirty dishes and clutter. Robert felt he needed to go down the hallway toward the bedrooms. He'd been informed that the death had occurred in one of the bedrooms. So far he felt nothing but good things and family fun.

He went down the hall and was drawn to the bedroom on the left.

Sheila was filming their surroundings, likely wondering when Robert's dark vision would kick in and how she'd recognize it when it did.

Once he got to the open doorway, Robert heard a soft snoring. When he and Sheila walked into the room, he saw a young Black woman lying on the bed asleep. She had on some pink pajamas and was under a sheet. A cooling ceiling fan slowly spun above her in the center of the room. On her dresser was a mirror with a picture of her and a boy and a girl. Beneath the picture on a white border was written "Tanja, Jasper, and Haley."

Suddenly there were heavy footsteps behind them and the killer slowly walked into the room. He paused and briefly looked at the pictures on the dresser. He approached the bed, leaned over, and gazed at the young woman.

"He's here," Robert said.

Then the man sniffed deeply, like Robert had seen him do before. He put his right knee on the bed and then straddled the woman, setting his left knee down on the other side. She awoke with a start and looked up at him and suddenly panicked and began striking him with her fists.

"Who are you, and what are you doing in my house!" she yelled. "Get off me!"

The man chuckled and grabbed her wrists, secured them both in his left hand, and held her tightly. He punched her in the head once, and some blood ran from her nose and mouth. She yelped from the pain.

He reached behind him and pulled a large knife from his belt. You could see her trying to figure something out—some way to escape.

"Please, sir, I have children in the next room! Please don't kill me! I beg you! I'll do anything you want!"

He took the knife and sliced her pajama shirt from the neck down and yanked the shirt open, revealing her breasts. She became quiet. He smiled and touched her stomach, then felt her breasts. She didn't struggle as he did so. She didn't stop whimpering and crying softly, but she was trying to calm him down.

The man wanted her to be frightened and attempt to fight him off—that seemed to be one of the things that got him off. She would do anything to protect her children. He leaned down and licked the side of her face twice. Then kissed her, and she hesitated but then returned the kiss. She tried to use her tongue to kiss him back, and that made him mad. He raised back up and punched her in the face twice. She appeared to be unconscious. He pushed her face around a few times, and she made no movements.

He climbed off her and reached down to pull off her panties and pajama shorts. She moved suddenly and kneed him in the chin, and then extended her right leg and kicked him in the chest. He stumbled backward toward Robert, and the woman tried to jump up and push him aside to flee.

He shook his head and grabbed her before she could get out of the room. Then he threw her back on the bed and climbed on top of her again.

"You little bitch! You're going to die, and I may go after your children too."

He picked up his knife and thrust it into her chest, then pulled it out and thrust it in once more.

The killer flipped her over on her stomach and stabbed her in the upper back twice, and she yelped each time. Laughing, he ripped off her thin shorts and panties. He then rolled her back over, grabbed her neck, and sliced her throat, just like he had the others, when there was a sudden noise from the other room.

The man turned his head toward the noise and stepped back off the bed.

"Stop, you bastard!" Robert yelled. "Not the children! Leave them alone!"

The killer suddenly turned in Robert's direction with a confused expression on his face and began to wave and jab the knife toward him. He moved it around as if he thought there was someone there who he couldn't see. The knife waved very close to Robert, who subconsciously moved back just a step even though he knew the killer couldn't possibly cut him. He just didn't understand how the man could even sense him.

The man was spooked for some reason, because then he grabbed a bracelet off the woman's nightstand with little trinkets of a boy and a girl. He tossed it into his pocket and walked toward the door, but then he turned and came back. He quickly sliced off a section of her hair, placed it in his pocket, and once again headed for the hallway and door.

The kids were making quite a bit of noise at this point. Robert wanted to go in there and check on them, but he knew they weren't there. The killer walked towards the front door.

"Oh my God!" Robert yelled, and then the gift collapsed around him and he sank to the floor.

He wondered how long she'd lain there with the kids in the next room before she was found. He also hoped that the kids hadn't seen her like this. Sheila set the camera down and grabbed Robert's shoulders and held him. She could see that this vision had completely devastated him.

He began crying, and she held on to him for a couple of minutes until he settled down. This had been a horrific scene. When Robert stood up, Sheila continued to hold him to help him walk out. He pushed the kids' room door open, and the room was empty.

"Thank God he didn't go after the children," Robert said.

He turned back and looked into Tanja's room, and everything was missing there, too, except the bed, which had a bloodstain on the bare mattress. Then he noticed the photo of Tanja and the kids lying on the floor. He picked it up and placed it in his pocket.

When they were outside again, he started to explain something to Sheila, and she told him not to talk right now.

The police officer jumped out and came over when he saw Robert's state and asked whether he was OK.

"Sorry," Sheila said, "but he is clearly not OK! Please help me get him to my car."

Robert vaguely remembered Sheila and the cop helping him into her Buick. Sheila went to the cop and talked to him for a few minutes before returning to the car. She asked whether Robert was doing OK, and he replied that he was tired but all right. Sheila drove them to her house. Once they arrived, she helped him into her house to a bed and helped lay him down.

Sheila left the room, and Robert fell asleep almost immediately. Though, right before he did, he thought, *Wow, this murder really took a toll on me.* In the past, when he'd seen deaths, it had been very sad but left no negative impact on him or caused any nightmares. Witnessing people during a murder scene certainly bothered him more. He hoped the death journal he'd soon write would help him move past this, but from time to time, he would continue to think about each victim and scene.

The help Robert provided the families outweighed the negative impact on him. But he was not prepared for how much witnessing a violent murder like this would affect him. Seeing this most recent violent murder did cause nightmares, waking him several times. He might never forget these visions.

A while later, Sheila woke him up and had some food for him. She'd made some tacos and brought him some chips and a glass of wine. She pretty much fed him, and then he fell asleep again. The next morning, he awoke early and went through the house until he found her in the kitchen. He could hear her clanging pots and pans around. That was a great sound—reminiscent of his home when he was young. She had some coffee on and was making some bacon and eggs.

They didn't talk for a few minutes, and when she sat down, she asked, "Are you doing OK?"

"Thanks to you, much better."

"Does it always hit you that hard?"

"That's the worst I've ever had it!" he said and paused. "I wonder how this man picks his victims. Would he need to stalk them to learn their schedule and where they live, or do you think they're just victims of opportunity?"

"He has to choose them somehow," Sheila said. "I'm sure the police haven't looked into that yet since they thought they caught him. I'll see what I can find out."

"I'm being drawn into the gift at a much deeper level than ever before," Robert said. "Somehow the guy seemed to know someone was there. He waved his knife to try and locate me. I don't know how that's possible, since this happened in the past. That scares the hell out of me."

"I saw how you jumped back as though you were trying to avoid something."

Robert thought for a moment. "He didn't cut down Tanja's torso like the first two victims in my vision, and it seemed to be because he was somehow distracted by my yelling at him or the kids' noise in the next room.

"I want to know how long she lay there dead before she was discovered and whether the kids saw her or not."

"I'm sure we can find that out at the family meeting," Sheila said. "Even though I couldn't see anything, it still scared me. I'm so glad I was there with you when you came out of it."

"I may have to hire you to help me get through these investigations."

"Did it throw you off or cause you any problems, my being there? I tried to be as quiet as possible. You were in a trancelike state while that was going on. I could tell you were watching or experiencing something, the way you were looking around and moving." Sheila came over and ran her fingers through his hair and held his head against her chest to comfort him.

"No, you didn't distract me at all," he said. "I'm so happy you were there with me. I haven't had any friends in a long time. They become afraid of me."

She chuckled. "Yes, and I was worried at first about how weird you might be, until I started to get to know you and saw how passionate you are about these families and helping to solve these murders."

He laughed a little at that.

"I'm not afraid," she said, "but I understand what you're saying. I could see people being nervous around someone who can see people dying or dead. Are you OK being around me with my brothers being cops?"

"I'm happy we're together and that this doesn't scare you away. I have no problems with your brothers being cops."

For the remainder of breakfast, they tried not to discuss any further what had happened, so they made small talk about what each liked and didn't like. He told her that he thought this was the best breakfast he'd ever had, and she laughed at him.

He helped her clean up after they ate and then sat in the living room for a few minutes.

Then he asked, "Can you please take me back to the hotel so I can get started documenting what I experienced?"

She was quiet for a moment. "I have an idea I'd like you to consider. I have a spare bedroom, fast internet, and a printer if you need it. Why don't you stay here with me until this is done? I don't think this is going to get any easier for you."

Robert looked at her for a few moments and said, "Are you sure you'd be OK with that?" He hadn't even considered doing this.

"Robert, I think I can handle this. I think you're going to need me to help you through this, and I definitely want to understand what's going on here better. I am very strongly inclined to begin going to church again, though."

He agreed.

That afternoon, they moved his things, which wasn't much, from the hotel, and she had a spot on the street to park his Jeep. He put what few things he had in her spare bedroom. He wasn't accustomed to being around people other than family, so this was going to be interesting, but he was certainly grateful. He assumed there was nothing intimate about this situation yet. He called his family as he always did every two or three days and let them know he was staying with the PI who was working on the case, and they didn't even ask him whether the PI was male or female.

They know me, he thought.

He spent the rest of that day and the next in the spare bedroom writing up the entire event in his latest journal, sketching Tanja and the man and even drawing her bedroom the way it had been during that incident. The killer's trying to attack Robert had him concerned.

He didn't see me, Robert thought, *but he felt me. I don't understand that at all, and I need to try and figure that out. Maybe this killer has some sort of gift too. God, I hope not. That would be some sort of time shift. I am not going to let anything stop me, though. We are going to get him—no matter what.*

Since Sheila had a connection to the police, they were becoming more interested in what was going on, and they, too, wanted copies of Robert's *death journals* now. He was very glad to hear this. They would actually be using his drawings of the killer and trying to identify him, not because they entirely believed Robert yet but because it was the right thing to do. Since there had been no deaths like these since their suspect died, they still felt or hoped they had it right.

He began to think his detox would take a little longer this time. Robert called his mom and asked her whether Grandma had ever talked about any experience where someone in her vision had been aware of her being there. She did not, but she said she'd ask a couple of her old friends and family to see whether they'd ever heard of anything like that.

"I don't believe it's possible for that to happen," Mom said, "but this is the paranormal, and no one knows everything that's possible."

In the meantime, Sheila and Robert went on the internet and found nothing except for one story about a woman in North Carolina who'd had something similar happen on a paranormal site. He tried to locate the woman in the story, with no luck. This was uncharted territory. This didn't surprise him.

He figured he should be less conspicuous when they went to the next scene and see what happens. Sheila took Robert out and about the Pittsburgh area to show him some of her favorite places to go and things to see to help him unwind. They saw the Pittsburgh Zoo and Aquarium, which was great. They also went to the Frick Art Museum and park.

CHAPTER 9
THIRD FAMILY VISIT

On the third day, they were scheduled to meet with the families again to convey to them the experiences they'd had this time. They met at the Whites' home once again. They said it was a good, convenient location for everyone, and no one else volunteered to use their home. There was ample space in the room in which everyone gathered, and plenty of parking outside.

A few of Tanja's family were present. It was her mom and two brothers, the Hamers. Tanja was a single parent. The children's father had not been involved in the children's lives since Haley was born. One of the brothers, Dane, had taken Tanja's children into his home to raise them.

All these people seemed so kind. Robert remembered the photo that he'd picked up off the floor in her room and gave it to Dane for Jasper and Haley, and Dane thanked him. They were all heartbroken. Tanja had been a very good person who'd loved everyone around her, especially her children. This group was larger. It almost seemed too large now. Robert was concerned about that for some reason.

Mr. White once again started things off, which seemed to be fine with everyone. Once he had calmed everyone down and explained the process and introduced him, Robert began his story, with Sheila by his side, vouching for his actions. He explained the vision step-by-step, walking through the death journal and how he'd become concerned for the children.

He didn't talk about the killer acting as though he sensed him in the room. A couple of people who he'd never seen before seemed pissed off and left. He didn't care. Once Robert was done, Mr. White once again talked about the parts of the story that matched the crime scene evidence, the picture of the killer was similar to the others—it was clearly the same man.

Robert asked them who'd discovered Tanja and whether the children had seen her.

"I've been worried about that since my vision," he said. "I could hear them making noise in their room while that was going on."

Tanja's mother tearfully said, "I was supposed to go to Tanja's that next morning, and the two of us were going to run some errands together. I let myself in the house like I always do. I yelled out, 'Tanja, your mother's here!' I heard the children in their bedroom making noise playing, so I went there first, and then I began wondering where Tanja was.

"I opened her bedroom door and found her … like that." She gasped and began crying. "I was so shocked by what I saw, but thank God I thought of the kids. I called Tanja's brother Dane and told him to come over to Tanja's house right away, and then I called the Police.

"Dane called Devon and told him to go there too. I stayed with the kids until Dane arrived, and then he took over while I took the kids to my house. I wanted to get out of there before the police came and all of that craziness started, and I definitely didn't want them seeing their mother like that.

"Oh Lord, I will see that the rest of my life! My poor baby girl killed like that! Dear God, how can people do something like this?"

"I feel so bad for you," Robert said. "That is something a mother, or really anyone, should never see—but especially a mother."

He went over and gave her a big hug, and she hugged him back firmly, though she was shaking and crying.

She pulled back for a moment and looked him in the eyes. "I really don't know how you see these horrible, awful things happen as you do and keep your sanity. God bless you, honey."

They both continued to hug and cry for a few moments.

At the end, Mr. Dorsey, Rose's husband, stood and softly said, "They exhumed Rose's body and checked her nails and her cheek for DNA. There was tissue under her nails, but it was too degraded to match anyone, and it wasn't enough yet to exclude Tim Higgins. I thought we should all know."

"Thank you for sharing that," Robert said. "I know that wasn't easy."

Robert had a feeling the man he'd seen committing the killings had to have a record. He seemed an evil man—psychopathic, with no remorse. At the end of the White family meeting, Mr. White gave Robert the customary envelope regarding the next house as well as another envelope with some cash in it for expenses. Sheila was able to answer some of the questions now, so that was another benefit of having her with him. The two of them left and drove back to her house.

The next day, Robert's detox started OK, but Sheila came in with the newspaper and shared some disturbing news with him. Someone who'd been at the family meeting had gone to the news with a picture of him, and the news article revealed who he was and what he'd been doing.

"I'm surprised it didn't say where we're living," Sheila said.

According to Sheila, the article was pretty neutral about his powers. The paper neither mocked Robert nor praised him, and he was OK with that. But this was really bad since now he knew the killer hadn't been caught and they didn't know who he was. Robert felt he was officially a target.

He didn't read the story, of course, but there were three photo places on the page. Sheila began to read the story out loud, and he asked her not to do that.

"Sorry," she said. "I forgot."

He saw his photo labeled "Paranormal Investigator"; another featured Tim Higgins, "The Killer"; and the third image was a dark silhouette with a question mark. This was getting more troubling now.

Sheila and Robert did get out and talk walks, and they went to see a movie and pick up fast food to relax.

He really liked the walks they were taking. The weather was pretty nice. It was sunny and warm, with a nice breeze. They stopped by a Walmart and bought him a couple of pairs of shorts, some boxer shorts and jeans and a few T-shirts. He loved her company. He did have a couple of nightmares. One nightmare was about Tanja, and the other one included all three of the women.

After two days, Robert calmed down and was ready for the next house. He would be a lot more cautious during this visit. Two of Sheila's brothers, Michael and Jason, stopped by Sheila's house on the second day to try to talk Robert into stopping his investigation for his own protection. They explained that Tim Higgins had been a suspect because he had had a lengthy record of drug use, robbery, and rape and had been seen fairly close to two of the victims on the days of their murders. They said they were definitely looking into this other person more now. Robert talked to them about the tattoo the killer had, which they already knew about from his notes.

"Thanks for thinking of me," Robert said, "but I have to finish this now."

"I intend to work with him until the end now too," Sheila said.

"We'll have at least one officer at each scene," Michael said, "to try and catch him when he tries to kill Robert."

He said this with no smile. So they were pretty convinced that Robert was right at this point.

Sheila was watching Robert. "I'll make sure we get through this, and I'm glad the news didn't disclose where we are now."

Robert's family called his cell phone to see how he was doing because they had seen his picture on their local news, watched the story, and then found it on the news station's website. The Cincinnati local news knew more about him and had done a short bio about his gift. They sent Robert the link. There was an interview with his old girlfriend Teresa, who talked about his experiences at her mom's house in Hamilton, Ohio.

On the news story, Teresa said, "Robert Anderson and I used to date. One weekend, we went to visit my mom who lived in Hamilton

Ohio. We spent the day, hung out, and had dinner. When we started to leave, Robert saw a house two doors down from Mom's and couldn't take his eyes off it. My mom told him that house was the so-called murder house he was looking at. Mom told him about that terrible event on Easter Sunday in 1975, when a man who lived in the house lost his mind and killed eleven of his family members there.

"My mom and I continued to talk to Robert, but he was in some sort of a trance and didn't even hear us talking to him. He actually walked over to the house and looked in the windows. Those poor people that live there just want to be left alone. He told me he sees and hears ghosts. I decided I couldn't deal with that and broke up with him."

"I found the story about the mass murders on the internet," Robert said to Sheila. "The killer had a bad life. He likely suffered from some form of mental disability and couldn't keep a job, lived with his mother, and was abused by her. She put him down all the time and compared him to his brother. The killer was into drugs and was a violent alcoholic. They called it familicide. He killed his mother, brother, sister-in-law, and their eight children. Robert actually dated his sister-in-law first, and she left him for his brother."

"It was awful, and I'm so glad I didn't go in the house to witness it directly. I know there are murders across the world each day, but this was a bad one, and I would never go to that house again."

CHAPTER 10

THE FOURTH DEATH HOUSE

SHEILA TOLD ROBERT THAT SHE WAS WORRIED ABOUT HIM NOW. SHE was afraid he was nearing a nervous breakdown because of how deeply these murder scenes seemed to affect him and how difficult it was getting for him to recover from them.

"Maybe I'm beginning to like you and I know I'm worried about you." she said and smiled.

Robert smiled.

"Well," he said, "these scenes are more intense than normal."

She didn't know him that well yet, but she said, "You seem to be getting much quieter and more withdrawn."

He knew he was not her normal type of guy. She'd been brought up around police and military. She probably dated athletic and adventurous types of guys, and Robert was neither of them. Perhaps she felt like she needed to take care of him. She said she'd felt sad for Robert and what he'd been handed. But he didn't want her to like him because she felt sorry for him. Maybe they were just supposed to meet and work together and solve some of these odd, awful cases.

The next murder house was a few miles from the first house and about a twenty-minute drive from Sheila's house. It was a farmhouse on several acres. The grandmother, mother, father, daughter, and son lived on the property. The daughter had been murdered while home alone.

Robert intended to keep his distance a little better this time and simply observe. Sheila didn't walk behind him this time; instead she walked next to him and held his elbow.

There was once again a police car out front, and Sheila waved at him when she and Robert went by.

"That's my brother Jason."

Surrounded by cornfields, this house sat back off the main road a good distance. Weeds poked up occasionally from the gravel driveway, and two large trees stood close to the house. Robert knew that some farms planted trees strategically to provide shade and cool during the heat of the day. One of the trees was east of the house and the other the west, which would keep the home cool during most of the day.

It was a nice two-story brick house with a metal roof. Lattice covered the underside of the large porch, which ran the length of the front of the home. A red barn stood to the left rear of the house, with a fair-sized fenced-in area around its left side, where two horses were eating grass. A large doghouse was close to the barn.

As with most farmhouses, the front door and shingles were black and the windows were tall on the first floor. At one end of the porch, a senior woman sat in a white porch swing. She was not a ghost. Robert was surprised since no one was supposed to be home during his visit. He found out she'd just refused to leave but said she wouldn't interfere.

Sheila parked close to the house, and Robert didn't feel anything yet, but there was something odd about the two dogs. Now the dogs had moved close to the front of the house, and they weren't solid—they were transparent. Sheila kept looking at Robert.

As the two of them walked to the porch, the woman nodded and thanked them for coming. Robert asked her what her name was.

"Ethel Carol, like Fred and Ethel," she said and then held her hand over her mouth as she laughed.

She appeared to be in her late eighties, and her gray hair was pulled back tightly in a bun.

"It's such a nice day today!" Sheila said.

Ethel looked sternly at her and didn't speak. Then she turned to Robert. "I heard you have some powers and you see things."

"Yes, I have some," he said.

"I have some powers too," she said.

He nodded and asked her what she experienced, and she said she'd talk about that after they went through the house.

"Don't you have any dogs?" Sheila asked. "Most farms have dogs to keep other predator animals away, and we saw a doghouse."

Robert snapped his gaze around and looked at the two dogs again—now he understood they were ghosts, still trying to watch out for the family.

"They're dead!" Ethel said. "They died a couple of days before he killed my Lexi."

Sheila was taking notes. Ethel told Sheila and Robert that they should go in and do what they had to do. He knew the young woman had been murdered in the basement. They opened the front door, which squeaked upon moving. He began hearing the undertone of laughter and joyful times around him, and the feeling was positive. It made him feel good, and he smiled.

"There have been some happy times here," he said to Sheila.

Sheila smiled, too, as she watched him and began recording with her video camera. They slowly walked around the ground floor, first the living room, then the dining room and the kitchen, but the happy tone had only hints of darkness.

He could hear a man raising his voice. He could hear a kid afraid and crying. He walked over and looked upstairs and sensed mostly good feelings.

Along the wall up the stairs hung framed family pictures, spaced evenly apart. A man—the father, Robert assumed—appeared in several of them and struck Robert as being full of himself, or maybe it was some sort of aura.

His daughter was right by him in the family pictures, with his son on the side and his wife almost behind him to his right. Ethel was in one of the pictures that contained the entire family. The wallpaper design was pretty, and all the wood trim had been painted white.

"We need to go upstairs," Robert said.

They climbed the stairs, and one of the bedrooms was drawing him down the hallway.

"Here we go," he said.

He slowly opened the door but remained in the hallway. The wave of vision quickly enveloped him as he stared into the room.

He could see the young woman sitting on her bed listening to music through headphones and moving her bare feet to the beat. She had a nicely decorated room. She was flipping through a magazine, and Robert could tell she had no idea something was about to happen. She would occasionally hum or sing lightly to the music.

Robert heard a creak on the stairs, and he pulled Sheila off to the side so they were out of the way. The big man slowly ascended the stairs and walked to the girl's bedroom door. He was the same man from before, but he was wearing different, dark clothes. He had a sledgehammer in one hand and a knife in the other.

He stepped through the doorway and moved toward the young woman. Robert followed him in but stayed close to the door and to the side. Because of her headphones and her concentrating on the magazine, she had no idea he was here until he was upon her.

She looked up at him and first smiled and asked, "What are you doing here?" Then she noticed the sledgehammer and knife and sat back on the bed, her smile gone.

"She knows him," Robert said.

Sheila continued to videotape, so he knew she'd captured what he'd said.

The killer slowly moved to her. "You are just like him," he said.

"Just like who?" she asked fearfully, her eyes large. It looked like she was beginning to move to get away from him.

He quickly raised the hammer, and though she brought her arms up to her face to block him, he was too powerful, striking her head with ease. She fell back unconscious, and blood began running down her forehead. The man pulled her headphones off, momentarily put them close to his ears, and then he laid them on the bed.

"Check the headphones for fingerprints," Robert said.

The man then picked her up and carried her toward the bedroom door. Robert and Sheila followed behind, but they needed to keep their distance as he walked downstairs with the girl draped across his forearms. He didn't appear to be aware of Robert yet. On the first floor, the man opened another door, turned a light on, and then carried her down some more steps.

"He knows this house," Robert said.

Still in his vision, Robert followed him down into the basement with Sheila close behind. A washer, dryer, and shelves were straight ahead. There were two small windows and a set of steps that led out of the basement, with doors closed over an outside egress, like storm cellar doors.

The killer turned to the right and laid Lexi on a bed that was there.

As Robert looked around the room, he said, "It looks like someone has been staying here, but not recently."

In addition to the bed, a sink and a toilet made up a small living space. A television sat on a dark brown dresser in front of the bed, and a medium-size area rug partially covered the floor. The entire room was fairly dark. The man did not turn a light on.

Lexi was beginning to wake. The man stood over her and began to touch her body through her clothes and smiled at her. She began pulling back, trying to avoid his touch.

She felt her head. "Look what you've done, you asshole! I'm bleeding!"

He then held her down with his left hand and took his knife and sliced her shorts and T-shirt up the center, as he had done before with the other women. She began whimpering softly, afraid of what he might do now. It took a few yanks for him to pull her clothing completely off her, and then he resumed touching her.

"Oh my God, stop!" she said. "Dad is going to kill you for this."

She appeared to be in her late teens and a very pretty girl with light brown hair and an athletic body.

"I think he is about to rape her," Robert said softly.

The man took her right hand a couple of times and brought it to his crotch. She kept yanking it back.

"What are you doing! That's disgusting!"

He kept leering at her and smiling as he touched her. She suddenly began screaming and scratching at his arms.

He's trying to get sexually stimulated, Robert thought, *but can't get there.*

He suddenly growled deeply, turned and picked up the hammer, and hit her three times in the head. Lexi was bleeding profusely now and was unconscious again. He put his fingers in her mouth for a moment and then took them to his mouth to taste them.

He grabbed the knife again and started lightly trailing it up and down her body. He stopped at her nipples and her belly button and eventually moved to her vagina for a moment. He wanted each person to be extremely afraid, terrified of his treatment, but she was unconscious now. He then trailed on down to her feet and toes.

Finally, he took the knife up to her throat and sliced her fairly deep from ear to ear. The blood spurted from her carotid artery, where the greater blood pressure was.

Robert lost himself and yelled out, "You just killed this poor girl, you scumbag, and I hope you die a miserable death!"

Sheila grabbed Robert's arm as he tried to run at the man, who suddenly turned and stared around the room. He knew someone was there. He smiled and licked the blade of the knife on both sides like he'd done before.

If I could kill him right now, I would, Robert thought. *I know there's no chance I can do anything to him.*

The man then turned and cut Lexi from her throat to her vagina. He reached and yanked a gold cross on a chain from Lexi's neck and placed it in his pocket. He cut a lock of hair off her head, and with the knife and hammer, he turned. Before he'd walked away, it all disappeared. Lexi had died.

This was the clearest vision Robert had ever experienced. This poor girl! Lexi's body was gone and the other furniture too. Thank God Sheila had grabbed him. Robert had almost run at him, which would have served no purpose. They looked around the room some more and headed for the steps. They walked up the steps and out the front door.

Ethel looked at them, and they stopped. She stared at Robert for a long moment.

"You saw him kill her," she said.

He nodded.

"God," Ethel said, "I wish I'd stayed home that day."

"I'm so sorry," he said.

"God bless you."

"This is someone in your family, isn't it?" Robert said. "Tell us who it is!"

"Yes, he is."

"Who is it?" Robert asked. "You need to tell me! You can save lives!"

Ethel didn't answer. She got up and walked inside the house.

They walked slowly to Sheila's car, got in, and started to drive away. She waved at her brother in the police car, and he waved back. Robert looked at the police car and asked her to stop. They stopped, and her brother pulled up alongside them. Robert got out and went to talk to him, so Jason got out too.

"You're Jason, right?"

He nodded, and Robert told him that the killer was someone in this victim's family. He pulled out a notebook and began writing.

"The killer knows this house well," Robert continued, "and the grandma even admitted that he's a member of the family, but she wouldn't tell us who it was. I think he was staying in the basement some."

"I'll call Michael," Jason said, "and he can look into it. If you're right, this will be a huge break in the case." He paused. "I wonder why he would want to kill a family member."

"I don't know," Robert said, "but we'll soon find out."

Jason picked up the mic and called in to share the information.

Robert and Sheila got back in her car and began driving again. She asked him what had happened, so he walked step-by-step through the events.

"The killer would have raped her first if he could," Robert said. "He couldn't get an erection like I have seen him do before."

A lot of serial killers can't perform sex. That was part of the reason they got so angry and killed their victims, until they decided they liked to kill and that turned them on. They'd get angry because they couldn't rape, so they just tortured and killed. There were also a lot of killers who successfully raped their victims. If they were all the same, it would be much easier to find them.

Knowing Robert wouldn't want to go into a restaurant to dine in right now, Sheila stopped on the way to her house and picked up some Arby's sandwiches and a big chocolate shake each. Once they arrived at her place, Robert collapsed on the couch, and she set up a TV tray with his food. He asked her whether she minded his kicking his shoes off, and she said of course not. It was really odd being comforted by her. Robert had never had anyone do that before.

"He's part of their family," he said. "We're about to break this case. The grandma knows who killed her granddaughter."

"My brothers are definitely looking into it now," Sheila said.

They made some small talk, and each drank a couple of bourbons on the rocks, and afterward, Robert just fell asleep on the sofa. He woke from a nightmare in the middle of the night, sweating profusely, saying, "Please stop! Don't kill her!" Sheila shook him to fully wake him, and he grabbed her and hugged her tight. She took his hand, led him to her bedroom, and helped him lie down. She had on her pajamas and lay down beside him. He put his head on her shoulder, and he fell asleep with all his clothes on for the rest of the night.

The next morning, Robert woke first. He rolled over and looked at Sheila. She was beautiful. He didn't know how she would react—she might slap him—but he leaned over and lightly kissed her on the lips a couple of times. He pulled back and looked at her.

Without opening her eyes, she said, "Is that all you're going to do?"

He leaned in and kissed her again, this time much deeper, and then kissed all over her face. She wrapped her arms around his neck, and they went in for deep tongue kisses.

She pulled her nightshirt off, and Robert began to remove his clothes down to his boxers, which was all he usually slept in.

She grabbed his hand. "No, please—let me."

She pulled his shorts down, leaned down, and began kissing around his groin. Then she slowly took him in her mouth. She easily stimulated him to a full erection. He paid close attention to her breasts. Her nipples were erect and perfect.

Before he knew what was going on, they were kissing each other all over. It was intense. He thought her mouth and body were extraordinary. He helped her through her first orgasm with his mouth, and then he lay on top of her and they were making love. She pulled at him with her hands and wrapped her legs around his waist. It was amazing, and she wanted him to stay inside her, and she yelled when they finished together. They then both lay holding each other and fell back asleep.

"Wake up, lazy bones!" she called sometime later. "You have a story to write, and I have some video I want to pull together."

"Have you looked at any of the video yet?" he asked.

"Yes, I have," she replied.

After Robert got dressed, he went to work in the spare bedroom for a while. Eventually, he decided to take a short break.

"Perfect timing," Sheila said upon seeing him. "Want to check this out?"

"Sure," he said. "What'd you get?"

She took him to the sofa. Her video camera was hooked up to the VCR on her TV. The first video was of Tanja's house. They were walking into the bedroom. When the killer walked in, there was a gray misty outline of a form, a shadow, moving about that looked like where Tanja had been lying. There was no dark figure or shadow where the killer was, which didn't surprise Robert, because the man wasn't dead yet.

There was a shimmer that Robert realized later was her bracelet being taken from her nightstand, and the photo floating down to the floor, where he'd picked it up. There were some audio pieces that sounded like voices, but they couldn't clearly hear them. They could, however, hear what Robert had said, and see his response to the knife being swung at him as he pulled back.

The next video was in the farmhouse that Lexi lived and died in. A ghostly fog of an image appeared in front of them where Lexi had been suspended about where she lay on the bed, but of course, there was no bed or any of the other furniture in the video of the present day. The fog swirled about a bit as the man attacked her.

"Do you see that mist or fog?" Robert asked. "That's where Lexi was."

Suddenly there appeared on the TV a fairly clear image of the gold cross and chain being removed from Lexi's neck, as well as a momentary reflection of Lexi's face.

"Oh my God!" Robert said. "I've never seen this much on a video before!"

From there to the video's end, nothing else showed up—though that had been some really cool stuff, Robert thought.

He went over and kissed on Sheila for a couple of minutes before she lightly batted at him.

"You need to stop before we begin doing something again. Not that I don't want to, but you need to go finish your death journal."

"Of course," Robert said. "You're right. I'll see you later."

Then Robert retreated to the spare bedroom to continue recording his vision and drawing the images. Sheila had a nice computer and printer, but he still preferred to do the entire thing on paper. It connected him better to the event. He made sure to capture things that he may have touched in the house and as much detail about the hammer and knife as possible. He had a solid recollection when he did this— he almost felt like he was there at the scene again. He never wrote anything about what Ethel had said, or the videos Sheila had captured, just every detail of the facts as he saw them, like he usually did.

He finished up the death journal the next morning, and they went out for a walk in the woods, which was very nice. She held his hand a lot when they walked. They stopped a couple of times and kissed too. She'd brought some picnic snacks for them, so they went to the top of a hill on a rock and sat, looking out over a valley, eating slowly and drinking some wine. It was such a nice day. He wished there could be more like this. He began to wonder what was going to happen after this was over.

Robert knew they hadn't known each other long, but he asked her, "How do you feel about us so far?"

She smiled. "I like us together. That's funny—I was going to ask you the same thing."

"You know, we make quite a team."

She nodded and said she'd thought that too.

We could do a lot of good together, Robert thought.

"With your skills and my PI knowledge, we could do a lot of good for families."

"I agree," Robert said, "and we need to talk about that some more after we catch this guy."

Sheila laughed. "So now you want to catch this guy too?"

"Why not? Someone needs to get him off the streets."

They watched the clouds and the birds flying by for some time before they decided to head home.

Sheila told Robert that she had talked to her brother Michael and that he'd gone to question the Carols about the killer being in their family. They'd told him to talk to their attorney. Mr. Carol had said they were crazy and that it couldn't be anyone from their family. Michael had done some research and had a pretty good idea who the killer might be.

CHAPTER 11

MEET ALBERTO BLACK

THEY SCHEDULED TO MEET THE FAMILIES THE FOLLOWING DAY. Because of what had happened following the previous meeting, the families had limited the number of people who could attend this time. No one talked to the news. They met at the White family's house again. Everyone milled about and met one another, except one man, who seemed out of place. Robert had never seen him before, but he seemed very nice and stared at him quite a bit. The man wore a dark suit. This didn't make Robert nervous, because with what he did, he got a lot of stares.

Before the meeting began, the stranger approached Sheila and Robert.

"Hello my name is Alberton Black. I want to talk to you at some point about using your special skills or abilities to perform some work for me."

"Here's my card," he said, "and I'll reach out to you soon."

Robert replied, "Absolutely. We'll talk to you as soon as this situation has concluded."

Mr. Black shook Roberts and Sheilas hands then turned and walked away. He did remain for the entire meeting, though. Mr. White began the meeting, settling everyone down. He mentioned that the Carol family had joined the group over the loss of their daughter, Lexi. No one in the room except for the Carol family knew what Robert and Sheila were working on about their family member yet.

Robert went through the death journal and read everything aloud again, and they passed around the pictures he'd drawn. Lexi Carol's mother and grandmother were there and remained quiet but were crying and holding hands. The picture Robert had drawn of Lexi was very close to the poor girl's latest photo. And the man he sketched was getting better with each iteration. The mother confirmed that Lexi had had a gold crucifix around her neck that she never removed but that she wasn't wearing at the end, so this serial killer had taken another trophy and her hair too.

Sheila brought one of her brothers, Michael, who was the detective. He definitely wanted to talk to the Carols now. He still hadn't totally given up on their first suspect, and he was hoping this might help him see things differently. When they got to Robert's drawing of the killer in his journal, the Carol family didn't express much emotion except tears, and the man Robert assumed was the father, Mr. Frank Carol Jr., had tears running down his face. He remained stoic throughout.

He looked up at Sheila's brother and said, "I didn't want to believe the picture Robert had drawn was who I suspected, but with Robert's identification of the tattoo, I now had no doubt." The killer it seems is my brother, Arthur Lee Carol." There was a great mumbling among the group of people. Of course, it would be difficult to prosecute Arthur from Robert's drawing, but the family identifying his tattoo was enough for them to create a warrant for his arrest as a suspect.

"My brother, Arthur, has always had a mental illness. I can't believe he killed my baby girl. I should have done something more permanent about him years ago, but I didn't, and now she's gone. It's my fault she's dead."

Robert felt sorry for him during those few moments. Neither his wife nor his mother came over and provided any sort of sympathy or comfort to him.

"When Arthur was young," he continued, "it was evident that he had problems, and my father and mother tried to hide it at first, and then they tried to find a doctor to treat him. It was determined that he suffered from was manic depression, which is called bipolar disorder now, and suffered from sociopathy. There was no cure, and he would get worse.

"He was placed in a hospital and heavily medicated for years, and then one day, a few years ago, a doctor released him and said as long as he took his medicine, he would be safe to be around.

"You know how that works. They usually don't continue to take their medicine. He would come around occasionally and stay in the basement and then disappear for a period of time."

Frank Carol Jr. felt or hoped that Arthur would leave sometime and never come back, but he continued to come back, and they were all afraid of him generally.

"He had a bed in the basement and stayed there when he appeared. How am I supposed to live in that house now?"

Now the police had more than enough evidence to arrest him, but where was he? There was still another victim that they felt he had killed—unless he'd killed Tim Higgins too—and why hadn't he killed for a while? Robert wanted to go to Tim Higgins's murder scene next.

They finished up the family meeting. Michael cornered Frank and took notes as he talked to him. As soon as they were finished, the Carols left. The Carols never spoke to any of the other families. Michael approached Robert and Sheila and said he was going to find and arrest Arthur Lee Carol now. Robert answered all the questions the family members had today, and he and Sheila briefly talked to Mr. White before they left.

Now was his detox period again. He was even more anxious about this next visit. He had to be ready for anything from Arthur Lee Carol this time. He worried about Sheila going, even though, with her background and training, she could definitely handle herself better than he could.

They went back to Sheila's house to relax. They did talk for a while about what they were thinking about the Carol family and Arthur Lee Carol.

Sheila said, "Where does he think he is going to be able to hide now?"

"Well you know if he is truly psychotic, he isn't thinking clearly." Robert replied, "It's too bad that they could be normal if they take their medicine and don't. He is clearly intelligent, but insane on top of that."

They did their usual routine of eating and taking walks, and Robert had now more or less begun to sleep in Sheila's bedroom with her.

They didn't make love again during this time, but they kissed and touched each other a lot, which also helped him relax. She snored a little at times while she slept, and he loved it! They felt like they were getting along better all the time. They talked about their families more and possibilities for them. The weather remained a little cool and sunny, so taking walks was great. They were two days into his detox. Things were going well, and he was really loosening up—until another murder occurred.

Sheila's brother Jason called her and told her there had been another murder just across the state line, in West Virginia, which meant this time the FBI would be involved. They knew it was the same killer because the scene was very similar to the other scenes. Now everyone knew it wasn't Tim Higgins.

Jason felt like they were so close now and the FBI's involvement might slow them down, and it made sense: the FBI typically would start things all over again, and they might disregard everything Robert brought to the table. They had to hurry now and go to the Tim Higgins murder scene before everything exploded. This time both Sheila and her brother Michael would go.

CHAPTER 12

WE KNOW THE TRUTH NOW

TIM HIGGINS HAD DIED AT AN APARTMENT ABOUT A HUNDRED miles north of any of the crime scenes, literally on the north side of Pittsburgh. He'd had a history of drug use and violence. He had sexually assaulted three women that they knew about, but he'd died in a manner different from that of any of the women. He was apparently very high on drugs and shot himself in the head with a pistol.

There was no suicide note, but he knew the police were looking at him for the murders. Robert thought mainly he'd been at the wrong place at the wrong time. Tim had tried to live off the radar and kept quiet. Sheila and Robert packed up and rode with Michael to the apartment where Tim had lived and died. He'd lived in a unit on the third floor.

The building looked like an old hotel that had been converted into apartments. It was a large row brick building with a walkway along the doors on each floor and a rusty painted white wrought iron railing on the upper floors to prevent anyone from falling to the parking lot. His apartment was still vacant. It was clearly not in a great neighborhood, and with Tim's record, Robert wasn't surprised. It would have been impossible for him to find any employment with his record.

As they parked and exited the car, Robert was overwhelmed with bad vibrations—everywhere. He saw drug dealers, hookers, and homeless people around the area. He heard intense screams, cries, and moans all around, and sirens off in the distance. He didn't know what was real and what was part of his gift. He'd known this might be bad, but he had no idea just how bad. He thought this was what he'd sense in a war zone. He felt like he was waffling back and forth with the deaths and anger from all around them. Sheila noticed his unease and grabbed his arm to comfort him.

"Be glad you don't have my gift right now," Robert said. "This is a horrible, horrible place."

Michael shook his head and said, "I'll just stay at the car unless you need me."

Michael's nervous and doesn't want to be with me when I witness what I might witness, Robert thought.

There was no elevator, so Sheila and Robert walked the stairs to the third floor. Each floor had a door that was closed for the hallway. The stairwell smelled of old urine, and cigarette butts lay here and there, with trash all about. Robert could hear people shouting throughout the building and tried to remain calm. Sheila had gotten a key to the unit from Michael and as they approached the apartment door there were still remnants of crime scene tape stuck on the sides of the door. Robert knew now that he could never have done this by himself.

Sheila opened the door to Tim's old apartment, and they entered. All the furniture had been removed, and the unit had been cleaned—the harsh chemical smell hung in the air. Robert had no idea yet what had happened here, but he hoped to find out soon.

They walked around and explored the bedroom and bathroom for a few minutes, waiting for his vision to kick in. There had been so many bad experiences around him it was layer upon layer, making it difficult for him to experience this one event. It was like a nightmare blur. People would appear and then disappear. He saw women and children being yelled and struck. He even heard gunshots and thought he saw a fire for a moment. He had to get out of this chaos and go to the right vision or he might have to leave.

Robert finally stood in the middle of the room with his arms extended, and he felt it creep up on him. Sheila was right by his side as it went, but he no longer saw her. She was once again running her video camera, hoping to catch something. Suddenly Robert saw furniture appear and Tim come in the living room from the bedroom. He seemed to be nervous, pacing about, and Robert felt like the drugs had him agitated and frantic too.

When Robert had first begun experiencing this and a deceased person walked into the room, it frightened him. Tim was clearly high from something. He was shaky and staggered a bit. Suddenly there was a knock at the door, and he walked over, opened the door, and carefully peeked out—no one was there. He looked around and closed the door. A couple of minutes later, another knock came. Tim once again opened and peeked out the door, but again, no one was there. He shook his head. "Damn kids!"

The third time it happened, he opened the door and started to yell, and he was shoved backward into the apartment.

A large man in sweatpants and an oversize hooded jacket walked in.

"Who the fuck are you?" Tim said.

The man laughed an all-too-familiar laugh and pulled his hood back. It was Arthur. He pulled out a small vial of something, shook it, and looked at Tim for a moment with a cocky smile on his face.

Robert believed Tim wondered why this person had come to share some drugs with him. Drug users didn't always think clearly.

"I heard the police are looking for you about those girls," Arthur said, "and thought you might want to party a little."

"I haven't had anything to do with those girls—not that I wouldn't have fucked them if I had a chance. Why would I take drugs from you? I don't know you, fucker!"

Arthur stared at him, and a smile crept on his face. "Come here and hit this shit."

He headed into the bathroom, and Tim slowly followed him. Tim picked up a hand mirror from the vanity and sat down on the toilet.

Arthur walked over to him, and Tim held the mirror flat while

Arthur poured a couple of lines of his drug on it. Tim looked at it and with a big smile used another small mirror to straighten the lines.

Tim looked up at Arthur and smiled. "All right! That's decent of you, man." He paused. "Who the fuck are you, anyway?"

He raised a rolled dollar bill and began to sniff the drug.

While Tim concentrated on snorting the drug, Arthur said, "Death!"

Arthur quickly pulled out a pistol, stuck it to Tim's temple, and pulled the trigger. Arthur wore a glove different from the one Robert had seen him use during the previous murders. Tim's head snapped, and he fell backward into the bathtub, twitching for a few moments before becoming still. Arthur then put the pistol in Tim's hand, squeezed it, and let the pistol fall into the tub beside him.

Arthur poured the rest of the drug onto the mirror and sat it on the countertop with his other gloved hand. He pulled up his hood and walked out of the apartment. The vision disappeared moments later as Tim died. It had all happened so fast. Robert told Sheila what had happened, and they went into the hallway to understand how Arthur hid when he knocked on the door.

They didn't understand why Arthur had done it that way. Tim's apartment was the first unit on the floor, and there were two corners close to his apartment that would have been easy to duck behind. Maybe Arthur didn't think Tim would let him in so he tricked him to force his way in.

They had Sheila's video of the apartment to look back on—hopefully something unexpected would show up like on the other videos. Robert felt having a video of these places would also be useful if he needed to remember what each place was like.

They left the apartment, locked the door, and began heading down the stairs. As they passed the second floor, the door suddenly opened behind them, and an arm reached out and grabbed Robert by the neck and tried to pull him back into the hallway. Sheila didn't hesitate and hit the man very hard in the face with her fist, then began hitting his tricep, which caused him to release his grip.

He then tried to slash at Robert with a large knife and got his collarbone and down his chest, but it didn't penetrate through his jacket very well. Sheila then attacked the man again, and he dropped the knife. Arthur pulled back and slammed the door shut. Sheila quickly grabbed the door handle and tried to push the door open, but something was blocking it and wouldn't allow it to open.

Robert began coughing from the choke Arthur had performed, and he gripped his knife wound.

Sheila immediately called her brother. "Michael, Arthur was waiting for us and attacked Robert from the second-floor hallway!"

"Get down here to the car ASAP! I'll call the local police, but I'm going to begin looking for him!"

They ran downstairs and got to Michael's police car.

Michael was already gone to try to find Arthur with another local police officer. Sheila grabbed Robert and began looking him over.

"I'm OK," he said. "It's not that bad, thanks to you. I'll probably have a decent bruise on my neck, and I have a small slice on my chest."

It wasn't very deep but bled some. Her brother had called the paramedics too.

"We need to make a big deal out of this," Michael said, "to make people understand what's happening here and not overlook it."

Robert understood.

The police stormed the area. They blocked off a huge section to try to catch Arthur, and they remained there later into the night. Sheila and Robert had to go to the closest police station and file a police report.

It was the next morning when they finished, and Michael drove them back to Sheila's house. An unmarked police car followed them to Sheila's place too, and there was a cruiser in front of her house. The FBI stopped by later. They said they'd been following the case the entire time and were glad Robert was helping and making some progress. They felt like he was a big help in solving this.

The FBI agents were Stephen and Regina, and they asked Sheila and Robert whether they could accompany them to the last two crime scenes—one of the previous murders, as well as the recent murder in West Virginia. They told the FBI that they would of course go as long as Sheila could be a part of the work. Robert explained to them that she kept him grounded and had saved his life. He also wanted to visit the earlier death first. They agreed to his terms.

CHAPTER 13

Robert told Sheila that he owed it to the families who'd brought him here to summarize and share with them what had happened at Tim Higgins's apartment. She agreed. They ordered some dinner, and she drank some Robert Mondavi wine while he drank some Woodford bourbon and began to write once again.

This crime was clearly different, but he still used the same format he'd used before. He walked through the entire vision and drew pictures of the apartment and both men. The story probably wouldn't help the families much since they knew who the real killer was now, but he felt they deserved to know every piece of information he could give them. This would confirm what they'd been thinking all along and how Arthur had managed to stop the police from looking for him.

Sheila contacted Mr. White and scheduled an emergency family meeting for two days later, and he said he would reach out to everyone else. She quickly summarized for him over the phone what had happened to Robert. Robert stayed in the spare bedroom the entire next day to document the visit in his journal and definitively fill in some gaps. Sheila grilled some hamburgers and made some potato salad, which she brought into him when she was done. She came in one other time, sat on his lap, and kissed him for a while.

The morning of the family visit, Robert and Sheila got up early and grabbed some breakfast. He was really beginning to enjoy sleeping with her. Sheila went with him into the library this time and helped him make copies to take to share with the families. Robert had a creepy feeling while they were in the library, and he looked around for a bit, trying to figure out what was bothering him.

Then they drove to the Whites' house and met with the families. Even fewer people were present than before. Robert believed everyone had started to feel like it was close to being wrapped up and they knew they were right about the killer. Michael and the two FBI agents were there, but they remained quiet.

Mr. White wasn't present this time; the others said he wasn't feeling well. The Carols didn't show up either, which didn't surprise anyone, though a lawyer representing them had come, and he took a copy of the death journal to share with them. Sheila began and led the meeting until it was Robert's part. The families absorbed all the information and took their copies. Everyone knew what was going on now.

Alberto Black was there once again, too, and stared at Robert and Sheila throughout the family meeting. He seemed to study Robert as though trying to understand him.

Toward the end, Michael spoke up. "Arthur is a psychopathic serial killer, and we will get him."

At the close of this meeting, the group had very few questions.

Robert took only a brief detox this time. Sheila really quelled his anxiety. The two of them spent some time making plans for the last two events. They felt Arthur would try harder to come after them now that they'd exposed him. During the detox, Sheila took Robert to a pistol range and gave him instructions on how to load and shoot a semiautomatic pistol. He'd shot guns when he was younger, but it had been a long time. It was a lot of fun, and at this point, having a gun was a great idea for protection. He'd never felt as though he needed one before, but he certainly did now. Sheila gave him a small pistol that could be concealed in his pocket or on a belt strap.

CHAPTER 14

ARTHUR LEE CAROL

When Arthur left the apartment building, he was very angry. He'd parked his car a couple of miles away in a quiet area, and as he walked along in the dark, his anger intensified. He'd thought he could ambush Robert Anderson, kill him, and continue his task.

He'd killed his niece, which had been one of his primary goals. She was his brother's favorite, just like his brother was favored by his dad, that evil son of a bitch. He wanted his brother to hurt.

Dad never liked me and always favored Frank, Arthur thought. *I had to be born looking like Mom. She's the one who caused Dad's hate for me. He was still an evil man, but if I'd looked more like him, he would have had two favorite sons.*

He'd enjoyed killing Lexi. He wished he could have fucked her too. He'd enjoyed killing each of the women, but he'd enjoyed Lexi the most. They each made him feel better for a bit, but he didn't know what it would take to satisfy him completely. For some reason, he wasn't capable of sex anymore with a woman.

When Mom started refusing to have sex with me is when I stopped being able to have erections with these other bitches. She always felt bad for me growing up, not having friends or a girlfriend, and for how bad Dad treated me. Plus, the only time Dad wanted her was when he couldn't meet one of his female friends from work or from the bars.

He felt bad about killing women who'd had children, but he felt they were better off.

Police cars sounded in the distance. The streets were dark, and Arthur thought it might rain. *Maybe I could stop at a bar and have a drink*, he thought. But someone always bothered him, and he'd have to leave—plus a picture of him might be on TV now. He couldn't afford to draw attention to himself.

He could see his old car in the distance, and just as he approached a dry cleaner's, a young woman stepped out of the business and started heading in the same direction he was going. She was only a few steps in front of him, and she never looked back. She must have felt safe here. He thought it was perfect timing, like the others. When he felt like he needed to kill someone, they just showed up in front of him. Sometimes he would follow them someplace and then grab them, but he was very strong and knew he was scary to look at.

As she began passing his car, he jumped on her, hit her hard in the head and knocked her down, and threw her in the passenger's side. He loved to hit them! He didn't bother looking around to see whether anyone had noticed because it was getting too late for that now. Once he got in the car, he checked her out and knew she'd be out for a few minutes. He wrapped duct tape around her wrists just to be safe. He was going to have some fun with this girl.

He drove to the house carefully, always watching to make sure no one was following him. He pulled up to the house, and as he'd expected, she tried to fight him when he got her out of the car. He hit her hard, and she lost consciousness again. He picked her up and carried her in the house and upstairs to his bedroom. He would have to move the car to hide it later, but he needed to take care of her first.

When Arthur entered his bedroom, the other woman was still on the bed. She began whimpering and sobbing when she saw him. He laid the new girl down, and then he untied and dragged the other woman to the closet door and secured her to it.

"Shut up, bitch!"

As the new girl lay on the bed, he cut her clothes and removed them, and then he taped her to where the other woman had been positioned. Then he left and locked the room to go out and move the car to safety.

Upon reentering the bedroom, Arthur said, "I know you have to be awake now, new girl."

"My name is Bethany," she said.

"I don't need to know your name, bitch."

He walked over to the woman fastened to the door. "It's time for you to go now."

She began crying. "Please, no—I don't want to die. Please let me go, and I won't say anything to anyone. I don't want to be buried in the backyard." She looked at Bethany. "My name is Claire. God bless you!"

Arthur chuckled. "OK, Claire, let's go downstairs for some fun, and then maybe I'll let you go. Maybe you'll be better than the others."

He grabbed Claire and pulled her by her hair, and finally she yelled and stood up. Arthur walked her out the bedroom door, slammed it shut behind them, and locked it from the outside.

Claire was crying as they walked downstairs. A few minutes later, Claire could be heard screaming and crying. It seemed to go on forever, and then a few loud bangs occurred, and then silence.

Arthur enjoyed touching, kissing, and torturing the bitch Claire in the kitchen. She had been beautiful. After he finished, he decided he would wait until later to clean up the kitchen and find a place in the yard for her. He'd find a special place for her so that he could look out his bedroom window and remember her. He washed his hands and arms and face in the kitchen sink and then slowly went back upstairs to take a nap with the new girl. When he came in the room and once again closed and locked the door. He placed his bloody sledgehammer and knife on a table, and walked across and lay down on the bed with Bethany.

"Oh my God, is that her blood on your clothes?" Bethany said.

He grunted. "Let's take a nap before we get started. That made me tired."

He turned over toward her and placed one hand on her left breast, squeezed it, and held it. He seemed to go right to sleep. Arthur really had a bad odor, as though he hadn't bathed in a long time. His hair was greasy, and there was another smell of something else. Bethany never closed her eyes and lay there in terror. It would be impossible for her to sleep.

CHAPTER 15

FIFTH DEATH HOUSE - THE CAROL HOUSE

THE NEXT SITE WAS A SOMEWHAT RURAL ONE. THE YARDS WERE A little larger than normal, and a chain-link fence enclosed this house. The grass had been mowed recently, and the place was kept in good condition. Robert felt nothing bad when they pulled up to the property. They parked outside the fence along the front of the house.

The other homes in the neighborhood looked unique, so one could tell they'd been built by different contractors over the years. This families was a yellow-and-light-green framed wood house. It had a couple of small windows close to the ground, so it likely had a basement. Two white metal posts supported the modest front porch at each corner, reaching up to meet the small overhanging porch roof.

Sheila was watching Robert's reactions. There was once again a police car out front, but two officers were in it. This house was about thirty miles southeast of first house, where Carolyn White had died. Sheila and Robert looked around a bit before they got out of her car. She removed a pistol from her glove compartment and grabbed her video recorder. She holstered the pistol with a clip on her belt. "Did you bring your pistol in case we get separated?" she asked.

He smacked his waist where the holster was attached.

They opened the fence gate and stepped in, and he felt nothing bad. Not that gates or doors meant any sort of portal to a vision, but at times, he felt it was. In the yard, he felt and heard some happy elements of a family, with kids playing, but not much. Not experiencing bad elements or vibrations was a little odd, but not impossible. Nothing was really normal about this work.

They slowly walked around the house before heading to the porch.

"Have you picked up anything yet?" she asked.

He shook his head. "Nothing bad yet."

As Robert approached the front door, he still sensed nothing negative. He could hear muffled voices and some laughter, but not a lot. He turned the doorknob and opened the door slowly, revealing oak hardwood floors and some furniture in the living room. Sheila followed him in. The plank floors squeaked a little as the two of them walked across. Robert looked all around, and they began exploring each room.

The death was supposed to have occurred in the master bedroom. He should have felt something bad since he'd been a little reactive at the other houses. He so far registered only the normal happy family sounds. He began to wonder whether this was the right house. Even at the first house, he'd felt some bad vibrations during the first visit. He just couldn't enter his vision.

They were in the master bedroom, which still contained the bed. Robert turned to Sheila. "I don't understand it. I'm not experiencing anything sad or dark about this place—only happy sounds and memories so far."

They walked around once more, and the place seemed clean of any spirits or visions. They even descended into the basement and encountered nothing. Robert went out on the front porch and then reentered. He put his arms out in the bedroom where he thought the death had occurred, trying to push himself into the vision, and waited. He never felt anything bad, so he finally stopped.

They walked out the front door and went to the car. Sheila approached the police cruiser and told them that Robert hadn't experienced anything here and that they'd probably need to return later. After all, he hadn't experienced much at the first house until his second visit—and yet he'd still felt some bad vibrations among the good of those families who'd lived there, just not the murder. They would try to come back tomorrow, but Robert felt that something was wrong. They got in the car, and Sheila pulled out and turned around, and they began heading to her place.

About a mile down the road, Robert noticed a larger, two-story frame house tucked back off the road a bit. For some reason, he hadn't noticed it during their trip toward the murder house. It was run down but still a pretty house, he thought, when suddenly his gift hit him hard.

He laid back in the seat for a moment and felt like someone was holding him down by his chest. Sheila looked over at him when he gasped.

"Robert, are you OK? What's wrong?"

He caught his breath and yelled, "Please stop! Stop right now!"

She pulled off to the side, and it took him a moment to catch his breath. Pointing, he told her a murder had happened in this larger house tucked back in the trees.

As Robert stared at the house, a fog seemed to envelop it. He stepped out of the car, and Sheila ran around to his side.

"I have a very bad feeling about this house for some reason!" she said. "How can that be?"

She quickly grabbed her gun and camera and began filming the place. As Robert walked through the grass up toward the house, his vision became stronger with each step. He gasped a couple of times and almost wanted to turn around. The other house must have been a fraud. Someone must have been testing him or something.

Arthur was startled from his sleep by the sound of car door slamming and someone yelling. He jumped up from the bed and looked at the young woman. He wanted to play with her badly, but he had just taken care of the other bitch, and now it seemed maybe someone was here. *It must be that damned Robert Anderson and his girlfriend*, he thought. He had to get out of here.

"I guess we aren't going to get to play," he said.

He reached for his knife and began walking toward the woman. "I guess I'll just cut your throat and leave you here to let them find your dead body."

"Please, mister! Don't kill me!" Bethany said and started to scream.

Arthur's eyes widened. He knew someone was about to enter the house. He punched Bethany hard in the head to shut her up, and she did, but he knew he had to leave. He quickly duct-taped her mouth shut and went over to the doors to the deck. He looked back at the woman one more time and went outside to climb down the escape ladder.

As Robert moved closer to the house, his senses were on fire—the gift was becoming stronger and much worse. The large, windowed door wasn't closed. It was open about a foot, and then he had a terrible feeling.

He turned to Sheila. "Call your police friends and tell them they need to get their asses down here right now!"

She ran back to her car to retrieve her cell phone and made a quick call. She then ran back up to meet Robert, her pistol aimed toward the door. He moved forward to the steps and up to the door.

"Maybe we shouldn't go in there yet," Sheila said. "Maybe we should wait for them to arrive."

"I need to go in now," Robert said. "This is such a bad house!"

"Of course you do."

He entered, and there was a loud thump as the door swung back against the wall. Then he suddenly got a blast of despair and pain, and a pungent odor swept by him. It was as strong as a breeze, and the smell was one he'd encountered before—that of blood and death.

"Oh my God!" he called. "There's someone in here dead right now!" He placed his hand against the wall to steady himself.

The living room appeared to be normal for a moment, and then he began to hear a child crying and screaming. He heard a woman screaming in great pain, and a man, a father, was growling and yelling. He heard the sound of smacking and saw some of the furniture moving about violently. He heard a kid's laughter too. This didn't make any sense.

Then he heard sounds coming from other parts of the house. It was the same sounds of violence and evil. This house was evil! It was possessed by a family who had been tormented by evil. Robert was gasping for breath at this point, and he knew Sheila was close behind him, staring at him as his gift became stronger and he experienced the torment of this moment. None of the furniture was different in the dining room from before his vision had kicked in. Drawn toward the kitchen, he saw Arthur walking a naked woman from a doorway in the rear of the next room.

The woman had black hair and a black eye. Her lips bled, and her wrists were duct-taped together. She cried and struggled to walk, and Robert became so sad about what he knew was about to happen to her. She didn't fight Arthur at all. She seemed defeated and compliant.

He wondered *Arthur was here? Why was Arthur at this house?*

Robert followed them into the kitchen, where Arthur had lifted her up on the island countertop. She acted as though she'd given up. Arthur once again had a sledgehammer and a knife. He seemed a little different this time. Sheila followed Robert into the kitchen too and was clearly shocked to see the dead woman lying on the island countertop in the center of the room. She saw her naked mangled body spread on top of the island countertop. Blood was everywhere. Sheila was seeing it in real time, while Robert was witnessing the murder itself even though they were side-by-side. Arthur laughed loudly and he began touching her naked breasts, navel, and vagina. She seemed frightened but made no move as he touched her, perhaps hoping he'd decide to let her live. He removed his right glove and began touching her breasts and then playing with her vagina, taking his time and enjoying the moment. Then a frown came back on his face and he put his glove back on. He picked up the sledgehammer and the woman watched in horror as he began by hitting her hard in the head with the hammer. She raised her arms to try and defend against the blows to no avail. He raised the knife and stabbed her in the chest and began carving on her.

"Oh my God!" Sheila yelled. "This is horrible! Robert, don't touch anything! Please wait for help!"

He never heard her say that, and she grabbed his arm to hold him and began pulling him out of the room, back into the dining room.

He doesn't need to see any more of this, Sheila thought.

Sheila could see that the woman was black haired and had a nightmare expression on her face. There were some objects still lying on the counter that appears she was tortured with. A couple of her fingers had been removed. The killer had deeply sliced one of her breasts and cut the nipple off the other. Her throat had been bitten deeply and a piece nearly extracted. The killer had sliced the woman from her throat to her vagina and cut her throat from ear to ear. This was definitely one of Arthur's victims.

Robert knew she had been killed very recently. Her blood was still running and dripping from the counter. "This has just happened!" he called.

"I know," Sheila said, "and you don't need to see any more of this. She's still in the kitchen."

Sheila actually yanked and pulled him out of the awful vision and back to reality.

Sheila took Robert into the dining room and sat him down to keep him out of the way and to prevent him from seeing the kitchen scene.

She looked at him and said, "Don't move!"

The two police officers from down the street ran into the dining room and told Sheila and Robert to stay where they were.

Sheila said, "There's the body of a young woman recently killed in the kitchen to the left! It's horrible!"

Weapons drawn, the cops ran to investigate.

"Holy mother of Jesus!" one of them yelled.

The other cop was a little older, and he began looking around while the first one called in to report the awful scene. After a short period of time, other police officers started arriving and moving around the scene, taking pictures of everything. The police were calling for backup and the crime scene unit. One of the police officers was fairly young, and after staring at the victim, he ran to the back door to throw up in the yard.

This house had older furniture. Everything seemed to have a layer of dust on it. In this dining room there was a china cabinet filled with dishes and some knickknacks. There was a painting of a mountain scene on one wall and some cows in a different picture on another wall.

Just from sitting there, Robert wasn't sure whether anyone lived in the house. But he eventually began to unravel some of the other evil in this place. Sheila was involved with the police and the death in the kitchen, and Robert slowly moved off into the living room and resumed experiencing the anger, frustration, and sinister vibrations.

Robert felt another type of vibration—one unrelated to the death in the kitchen. It must have been another death that had occurred at the house. He had no idea where Sheila was at this point, and she was clearly overwhelmed with what was going on. It seemed like every time another police officer came in, they wanted her to retell what had happened.

Robert was concerned that no one had begun looking at the rest of the house. He felt like Arthur could still be here somewhere. He sensed more bad experiences in this house. In the living room, he continued to sense the evil father and the family. It seemed like a normal living room, just like the dining room had seemed.

There was a dusty old sofa, love seat, and recliner with two end tables and a coffee table in the center. All the tables were dusty. The recliner looked the most worn. He wondered where the family was who'd lived here. They seemed to have gone and left everything as it was, taking nothing with them. In a brief vision, Robert saw an older man sitting in the recliner, struggling with his last breaths, gasping for air, and then dying. He wondered whether that was the bad father.

Across from the sofa sat an old console TV—an old tube TV like his family had had when he was younger. Robert didn't see a TV remote, so he believed it was from a time before remotes were used. It was a long room with two picture windows on the wall behind the TV. He could tell that this room had mainly angry and unhappy experiences in it too. It started becoming more evident that the father had been very abusive to a son and his wife. Robert had no idea whether any of this experience was related to the murder.

He suddenly felt a draw from the doorway at the end of the room. It was the doorway from which Arthur had brought the woman. He moved toward the doorway, and it turned out to be steps. Robert turned and looked at Sheila and yelled out, "Sheila, we need to go upstairs right now." She headed over to him immediately.

"We need to be ready," Sheila said, "because Arthur may be upstairs, and we know he'd kill you in a heartbeat."

They got to the steps and on the wall above them saw photos of a family. There was a consistent theme among them: in each photo that pictured the dad whom Robert had just seen die in the living room, the man's face had been covered with an *X*. His face was *X*'d out in everyone with black ink. In the photos with the whole family—dad, mother, and two sons—the dad always had his arm around the same son. It signaled the dad was proud of that son. That son was larger and dressed very similar to the dad, in much nicer clothes. In fact, he looked very much like the dad. The other son resembled the mother.

The second son stood a short distance away from the other three family members, or tried to. The favored son looked familiar, and so did the mom. The mother and the other son had what looked like forced smiles.

There were photos with the clearly favorite son by himself. There was a picture of him with a young female.

The two top photos had been removed from the wall, and the outlines remained where the old photos had previously hung. The favorite son really looked familiar to Robert. He suddenly realized it was Frank Carol Jr.—so this house must be where Frank and Arthur Carol had lived. This was the house they'd grown up in. So the man who'd been *X*'d out, who'd died in the recliner in the living room, was Frank Sr. That made such perfect sense.

Sheila and Arthur needed to talk to Frank Jr. and his mother once again. Arthur had killed the woman in the kitchen in the house where he had lived and perhaps was still living.

They got to the top of the steps and looked down the hallway. There were hardwood floors with an old carpet runner that ran the length of the hallway. A few more scenery pictures hung on the walls. He saw four closed doors in the hallway. Sheila stayed a short distance behind him holding her gun out. To Robert it felt like the hallway was vibrating.

Robert opened the first door, which led into what appeared to be an office. The room had nice furniture for an older home office. There were pictures of the dad in here, too, with other men, as well as a picture of Frank Sr. and Frank Jr. on the shore of a lake with their fishing poles and vests. In another picture, they held shotguns in the woods as young Arthur stood slightly behind them. Still another of the Franks with a car. Frank Jr. was behind the wheel, so Robert assumed it was his first time driving. Once again, Frank Sr.'s face had been *X*'d out in each of these.

They noticed something unexpected about the desk. There was an older desktop computer monitor and keyboard on the desk, and directly in the middle of the top of the desk was what looked like feces.

"Well, it looks like Arthur pooped in the middle of his dad's desk," Sheila said.

It didn't look fresh. Robert didn't experience much emotion in the room. He thought Frank Sr. had run a tight ship and Arthur probably hadn't been permitted in here.

Back in the hallway, Sheila opened the door across the hall, and it was clearly Frank Jr.'s room. There was a photo of him with his high school football team and cheerleaders. There was a picture of him in a baseball uniform too. It was a fairly nice high school boy's bedroom. The bed was still made. An older computer sat on a youth's desk.

The closet was about half-full of old clothes and shoes. A bowling ball, some baseball bats, and a couple of footballs were about the room. The curtains were closed. Nothing out of the ordinary was happening here. Robert thought the younger son had to be Arthur, and it appeared that Arthur had no resentment toward his brother, Frank Jr., or his mother. Arthur had enormous anger for his father here, but he did kill his niece. That was confusing.

Robert proceeded out into the hallway once again and approached the next door, which, upon opening it, he found were steps leading to the attic. He decided he would go there last. There was a lock on the door, but it was unlocked. He opened the door slowly, and it was certainly the parents' room. The furniture was from the same era as that of the first floor. The furniture was dusty here too.

There was queen-size bed, two dressers, and a large window with curtains.

Oh my God, Robert thought. The experience became bad again. He had flashes of the dad yelling and slapping the mother. The mother cried as he hit her, and she yelled and pleaded with Frank Sr. The father would curse and laugh, then slap her. The bed was half-made, but one side of the bed had been slept in recently. Outlines again indicated where pictures had been taken from the walls. The father's clothes were all gone, though hangers remained in his closet. Some of the mother's clothes were still here. Robert and Sheila looked around the room for any other details that might help. Then they returned to the hallway.

"This is going to be a bad room!" Robert said. "I'm a little concerned about what we might find up there."

"Take it slow and easy," Sheila said. "Don't go too fast."

Then they went next to the door to the attic. He dreaded going up there. There was clearly something up there setting him off. There was a door that locked in the hallway, and there was a second door mounted at the attic surface.

"Please stay close to me," Robert said, "and get your gun out."

Sheila quickly pulled her gun out and said, "Maybe we should get some of the police up here before we do this."

Robert kept going—he was not about to stop now. They slowly walked up the stairs to the attic's top door. He knocked on the door first for some reason, and they both heard a loud moan from above.

"There may be someone in there," Sheila said.

Robert felt the gift begin to envelop him again. Sheila pushed him to the side, opened the door, and stepped through to the attic floor. She held her hand up to his chest to get him to wait. She slowly squatted a bit and moved in circles, checking the room for anyone who might be there. He finally looked in the room and entered into several visions at the same time. There had been a few deaths in this room. Robert felt like his head was about to explode from the visions.

"This is Arthur Carol's room," Robert said, "and he has killed several women in here. There are at least three overlapping visions going on at once right now."

The way the visions were coming and going caused him to wonder where he was. There was a muffled moan once again. At first he thought the young woman across the room was a vision, and then realized she was real. She was naked and tied to a bed, looking frantic. He jumped up in and headed for the young woman.

Sheila jumped in front of him again and yelled, "Wait, damn it! We don't know if it's safe yet."

As Sheila cleared the room, Robert had to focus on the young woman while being pulled in and out of the visions. The room was a bedroom that spread across the entire attic. Pictures and notes were tacked on one wall above a cluttered desk, and a closet stood near empty, with just a few very grubby clothes in it. The floor was plywood, with a cheap rug lying on parts of it, and the slanted ceiling walls were roughed in drywall. They'd never been finished and painted. The furniture was crude and grimy. This had been Arthur's bedroom growing up. He was apparently still coming here.

"OK," Sheila said. "He's not here."

They ran to the bed, and Robert pulled out his old pocketknife and began cutting the duct tape off the young woman. When Sheila removed the tape from her mouth, the woman screamed and rolled her head about wildly. She was clearly scared to death.

"He was just here!" she cried. "And when he heard you outside talking, he went over to that patio door and disappeared."

Sheila ran over to the patio door and went out for a couple of minutes. She came back in and said there was a rope ladder attached to the deck—he was gone.

Suddenly other police officers burst into the room and began scanning the space as Sheila had done. Michael was the head of the group now.

"What's going on here?" he asked before realizing what this place was.

"I think this is the Carol family's old house," Robert said. "I believe Arthur has been living here and killing here too."

The young woman was loose now, and they gave her a blanket to cover up with. She was crying uncontrollably, and Robert pulled her to him and held her through the chaos going on once again.

"Who are you, and how did you get here?" Sheila asked the young woman. Then she quickly turned to Michael. "We need to get her to safety and an ambulance to get checked out as soon as possible."

"There's an ambulance here that she can go in," Michael replied.

One of the police officers took the young woman and led her out of the room, but not before she stopped.

She looked at Sheila and Robert. "Thank you so much! My name is Bethany. He kidnapped me last night, and you saved my life. He thought about cutting my throat before he left but didn't."

"We're glad he stopped and didn't hurt you," Sheila said.

Then, before Bethany left, she said, "There was another girl here when I first got here, and he took her away earlier. She said her name was Claire. She told me he was going to kill her and then me and bury us in the backyard like the others." Michael went over and whispered something to the cop who was going to take Bethany downstairs.

Then Michael and Sheila asked Robert about what he had seen up to that point. Soon Michael was on his mic on his shoulder, directing all the police officers present to get around back and look for Arthur—try to figure out where he was.

Then he turned to Sheila and Robert. "I told the officer with Bethany to try to prevent her from looking in the kitchen. I know she's going to understand that Claire's deceased in the kitchen, but she doesn't need to see that awful mess."

Robert spoke, and another police officer took notes the entire time.

"The Carol family lived here years ago," Robert said. "If you look at the photos in the house, Frank Sr.'s face has been *X*'d out in every one of them. The dad was very abusive to Arthur and his wife, and he died in the recliner in the living room. This room was Arthur's bedroom. He was still living here and killing here."

"The girl we just rescued," Sheila said, "said the girl Claire in the kitchen had just been killed in here earlier today. Claire indicated others were likely buried in the backyard, and Robert experienced several other murder visions in this room."

"Yes," Robert said, "and there some photos and handwritten notes on the wall over there, too, that you need to look at, and this is most likely where you're going to find the trophies he took from each woman he killed."

Several of the police officers were standing and listening now, shaking their heads with their mouths open.

"We have go to get this bastard now," one of them said.

Robert walked over to the patio door on the small deck and saw Arthur's hammer and knife. He guessed that in his haste, he must have laid them down and forgotten to retrieve them before climbing down the long rope ladder. Robert looked into the backyard. *Where the hell did he go?* he thought.

There was a large expanse of overgrown dried grass surrounded by trees. In the center, close to the house, was a fountain, as well as a small concrete pond filled with nasty green water. A small angel had once poured water from its hands into the pond. Robert could clearly see places where the grass was shorter and had been disturbed.

"If you look out this door," he said to Sheila, "you can see places where some of the bodies are likely buried."

She came over and took some pictures and told her brother. He made a quick message on his mic, and several officers began moving around the backyard as they pointed to where they needed to go. This was going to be a daunting, horrible task.

CHAPTER 16

THE HUNT

ARTHUR WASN'T SURE WHAT HE WAS GOING TO DO NOW. MAYBE HE would leave town and try to go somewhere and begin again. Maybe he'd go out into a forest and hide for a while. He felt like he shouldn't go to Frank's house anymore even though Mom still lived there. Frank had to know by now he'd killed his favorite kid. He would drive for a while and try to figure this out. He still had some money that his mom had given him—quite a bit of it, actually.

The car wasn't a new car, but it ran good, and no one knew about it. He'd stolen it over in the next county when someone had stupidly left the keys in it. He considered heading off to Canada maybe and starting up there again. Maybe he should just go after Robert Anderson again and kill him.

He hadn't known what was going on when he was killing a few of the women. He'd felt someone else was in the room, but he never saw anyone. Was that Robert watching his kills? How could he do that from the future? He should put an end to Robert to prevent him from doing that again—or maybe he should go after his girlfriend and kill her to hurt Robert.

Sheila and Robert took a day to recover from this diabolically evil situation, and then he began documenting what he'd seen at the old Carol house. He still didn't have the entire picture, but he had enough to understand what had happened. He and Sheila went to dinner and drank a bit more bourbon at a local restaurant. They were both very quiet throughout the meal.

When they returned to Sheila's house, two police cars were out front. One was across the street, and the other was farther down the street in an unmarked car. Sheila and Robert watched a little TV and then went to her bed. She snuggled up to him, and they went to sleep. He had some horrible dreams again, but he managed to sleep most of the night. The next morning, they had breakfast together, and then he went off to the spare bedroom. He spent the best of two days in there trying to piece it all together. He wasn't sure who he would be sharing this with.

At one point Sheila says, "You know I care about you and want you to stay safe right?"

Robert replies, "Yes I know." He looks down as if he's a child being scolded. I know when you are drawn into your gift you don't have much control oer your actions," she says. "Thank God you thought to get me to you before you began going upstairs. If he hadn't left you could have been killed."

He smiles and says, "Yes maam."

"Your gift forced us to stop here and find this place and we saved that young girls life by stopping. Who knows how long this could have taken to find if your gift hadn't kicked in. I suppose I am going to have to stay focused on you when we do this again." Hopefully there wouldn't be many more before someone caught and stopped Arthur. "I guess I could handcuff us together when we arrive at the next scene."

Robert smiles and says, "I didn't know you were into that kinky stuff?"

Sheila takes a moment to understand what he just meant and she suddenly smiles in return and says, "You have no idea." They both laugh at that.

How would they find this lunatic and stop him? They were a step ahead of the police because of his gift.

Sheila called and arranged a separate meeting with the Carol family for the next day. Michael and three other police officers were there too. Frank Carol Jr. was accustomed to leading the conversation, and when he began, Robert told him to please be quiet for a moment. His face reddened, and Robert could tell Frank was getting angry.

Sheila starts by saying, "We are so glad you all could make it today." We all would like to wrap this up as quickly and as safely as possible. Don't you agree?"

Everyone nodded and agreed.

Robert says, "Arthur has been living in your old family house. Did you know that?"

Frank looked down.

"How long has it been since any of you have been to that old house?"

"It's been years," Ethel replied.

"Well he's been living there," Robert continued, "and in addition to that, he's murdered women there too. In addition to the women he's been kidnapping and murdering in the other houses, there are some young women there too, and he's buried at least three, the police have found so far, in the backyard."

"We know that your dad was a very abusive person, except to you, Frank."

Frank glared at Robert. His mother looked down at her hands.

"We know Frank Sr. abused your mother and your brother, Arthur," Robert said.

"That's no excuse for your brother to do what he's been doing," Sheila said, "but we are sure that contributed to it."

"And we believe you have been repeating this abuse," Robert said, "which happens a lot. Do you have any other children, sir?"

"My name is Elizabeth," his wife said, "and yes, we have a son named Larry."

"No one has made any mention of your son yet," Robert said. "How devastated do you think he feels about losing his sister, or have you thought about that?"

Robert looked at Ethel. "Mrs. Carol, it was very clear walking through your old home that Frank Carol Sr. strongly favored Frank Jr., and I can now see a resemblance between you and Arthur." He turned to Frank. "I believe that has something to do with why he killed your daughter."

"I'll kill that son of a bitch," Frank said.

"We believe—no, we *know*—Lexi was killed," Sheila said, "because she was your favorite. And maybe you're unaware of this, but you're probably treating your son like Arthur was being treated."

"If any of you has any idea where Arthur is," Michael said, "you need to let us know now so that we can stop any further deaths and arrest him. If we find out later that you do know, you will be arrested as an accomplice since you would be misleading the police."

"We don't know where he is now," Frank said. "We knew he might be staying at the house. Please have sympathy for my wife, if not me. We did lose our daughter too."

"We understand and sympathize," Michael said, "but if you have any idea where he may be, or if he contacts any of you, you must let us know immediately. Here is my card with my cell phone number on it."

After Sheila and Robert walked out of the meeting with the Carols, Michael caught up with them and said, "We'd like to put you in a safe house until we catch this bastard. You are definitely both targets now, and I don't want anything like this to happen to my sister."

"Let us talk about it," Sheila said, "and we'll let you know."

Sheila and Robert went back to her house, and after they relaxed a bit, he intended to write up his journal for the other families. Sheila tried to argue that they didn't need to now, since they knew who the killer really was, but Robert wanted to finish this for them. It took him a day to write up this version, which should be the last one. They were both tired and burned out. The police put an officer in Sheila's house this time. It was Sheila's brother Jason. He slept or sat on the couch all night.

There had been another leak to the media somehow about this situation. They stated that Arthur Carol was the murderer and he was on the loose. They had an older picture of Arthur, along with one of Robert's drawings, which looked more like him. They provided an 800 number for anyone to call if they saw him or thought they did. The FBI offered a reward for information leading to his capture. They warned the public not to approach him, saying he was armed and dangerous and considered a serial killer. They talked about the houses where he had killed the poor women and where the old Carol family home was. Michael called Sheila and said people were out looking for Arthur now, trying to help the police locate him. He must really be in hiding now.

CHAPTER 17

FIFTH FAMILY VISIT

THE NEXT DAY, SHEILA AND ROBERT MADE COPIES AND MET THE families at the Whites' house again. Mr. White looked exhausted and as though he still wasn't feeling too well, though he greeted them with strong handshakes and head nods. He told them he'd had a heart attack but that it was minor and he was feeling better now.

"Everyone," he said, "please have a seat so that we can get started. In addition to our family, the White family, we have folks from the McKensey and Dorsey families."

They raised their hands.

"We have a member of the Hamilton family."

Tanja's brother held up his hand.

"The Branch family's dad is also here."

The man raised his hand.

"Unfortunately, the Goodwin family are with us now."

The father raised his hand.

"And finally," Mr. White said, "the Ross family is here, although their daughter was fortunately rescued by the police and Mr. Anderson and Ms. Flores. Bethany and her mom and dad have joined us."

Bethany was crying, but she did walk over and hug Sheila and Robert.

"The Carol family very smartly did not join us," Mr. White said. "In addition, the FBI has joined us now, too, since someone found another woman's death in West Virginia that is not on our list, and a gentleman Mr. Alberto Black is also here from a special interest company, whatever that means."

Alberto laughed and raised his hand.

"This very likely will be our last meeting," Mr. White said, "unless we get together in the future to honor our girls. I have contact information for each of your families, so I or someone else will reach out to you. Now, let's allow Mr. Anderson and Ms. Flores to explain what happened."

Sheila handed out copies of the death journal for the Carols' old house. Robert began from the beginning, with the visit to the wrong house.

"We don't have a resolution for Samantha Branch's death," Mr. White said, "where her body was found. Her murder didn't appear to you, Robert, when you visited the house."

Suddenly Robert understood. He looked at Mr. Branch. "I'm sorry, but I think I understand now. Sadly, she must have been killed at the Carols' house, and Arthur must have taken her body to the other house for some reason. I see the place where the deaths take place, so that's why I wasn't triggered at the first house. She didn't die there."

"There are several young women's deaths that I saw at the Carols' old house, and I didn't get a chance to identify them before we had to leave. I now believe that Samantha was also killed there. I'm so sorry for your loss!"

"We now know who the killer really is. The remaining women who were buried there will be identified from their DNA. These women haven't been identified yet, but they soon will be.

"If the police can catch him and bring him in alive, they'll hopefully find out much more."

It was a very somber meeting. There were clearly other families who should have been part of this meeting but weren't aware of it because their daughters' bodies hadn't been identified yet. Robert went through the rest of the experience, explaining everything he'd found in the Carols' house and how the police had responded. He described how they'd found poor Bethany just in time to save her life and how Arthur had escaped.

"I don't believe it'll be long before the police locate him and either arrest him or kill him," Sheila said.

He walked through the entire event until they left. There were a few questions, but not many.

After the meeting finished, Sheila and Robert walked over to speak with the two FBI agents and Mr. Black. Sheila had dug up a little information about Mr. Black that she and Robert had discussed the day before this family meeting. She found a website that revealed he was the head of a private corporation that specialized in cold case murders and rescuing families from criminals. They worked with police officers and FBI throughout the country to help solve these crimes.

The FBI said they should take a short break before they moved on to the remaining missing women's deaths. They still needed to identify who all the women were at the Carols' old house.

Mr. Black said he wanted to hire Robert because of his abilities. He said he was hiring other people with special talents and abilities, too, that were different from his to form a team to help people.

"I can pay your expenses for the rest of the time you're involved here," Mr. Black said to him. "After this is concluded we can discuss how we get started if you like. I don't want to place any more pressure on you than you already have."

"I'll only do this if you hire Sheila too. She's been an enormous help for me mentally and has protected me."

Mr. Black looked at her for a moment, smiled, and said he'd be glad to have her too. He'd already looked into her background and said she had some great skills to bring to his team also.

CHAPTER 18

After the family meeting, Sheila and Robert went to the police station where her brothers worked, and they met with Michael. He told them that they had found four bodies in the backyard. That made Arthur's total eleven, plus the one in West Virginia—so twelve that they know about. Michael said they hadn't yet identified the four women buried in the backyard.

Sheila told them they needed to talk to Frank Carol's mother, Ethel, and his wife, Elizabeth.

"I feel like they have a lot of information we need to know about Arthur and Frank," Robert said, "and what happened at that house that may shed more light on Arthur."

Time was of the essence now. They contacted Ethel and Elizabeth to schedule a meeting to talk to them about everything. They didn't ask to talk to Frank since he would have ordered his family not to share anything with them. They set up a meeting for the next day and proceeded to write down specifically what they wanted to discuss with the Carols. They decided to take a police officer with them too.

Michael said he wanted to put Sheila and Robert up in a hotel close to the police station to protect them for the time being. Sheila and Robert didn't want to go there but thought it might be best. They didn't want anything to happen to them either.

They went to Sheila's house and picked up some things. Robert clearly hadn't expected his trip to be so long and had to stop at a store and buy a few more shirts. They drove his Jeep and her car to the hotel just in case Arthur had seen Sheila's Buick, and if it stayed at her house, he might do something to her house if he could. They parked her car a distance away from any entrance at the hotel.

An undercover officer parked down the street to watch her house. The hotel didn't have a restaurant, so they ordered food and had it delivered.

During dinner, Robert said, "He may be long gone now. I would be if I were him."

"Well," Sheila said, "someone like him doesn't think normally, so he's not going to do what you and I expect him to do. He's likely looking for another victim—or looking for you."

"Is there a chance he may want to go after either his brother or his mother now?" Robert asked.

She thought for a moment. "That's always a possibility. There are police watching their house, too, just in case."

There were two queen-size beds in the hotel room, but Robert and Sheila intended to sleep together. They were getting comfortable sleeping together. Robert was a little jumpy during the night, but Sheila kept him calm.

The next day, they got ready and met Ethel and Elizabeth at the police station. The women had clearly both been crying. Stephen and Regina, the two FBI agents who'd been at the last family event, were there too.

"We miss Lexi so much," Elizabeth said. "It hurts so bad for her to be gone from our lives."

The others all nodded and said they understood.

Elizabeth looked at Michael. "Please—when are they going to release Lexi's body to us so we can lay her to rest?"

Michael told them that he'd talk to the coroner and see when they'd be able to do so.

"I'm considering taking Larry and leaving Frank and filing for a divorce," Elizabeth said. "This has all been a real eye-opener for me."

Ethel remained silent.

"Frank was trying to talk to Larry last night, and Larry, who isn't used to receiving any attention from his dad, didn't respond like Frank expected him to, which caused Frank to get mad. Larry got up and walked away from him."

Larry had told his dad, "My sister's dead now, and nothing's changed. You're still an asshole to me. You need to go away and leave me alone so I can miss my sister."

It would take some time and probably treatment for both of them to mend this relationship. They both had a lot to overcome. Frank was clearly upset with himself for how he'd handled this talk with Larry. He'd asked the two women to help him understand how to bridge that gap with his son.

"Larry is much smarter and more compassionate than Arthur was," Ethel had told him, "and if you keep working on it, he'll come around. But you need to let him grieve for Lexi right now."

Neither of the women had any idea where Arthur might be at the moment. They said he'd talked about moving to Canada in the past.

"Do you know of any place in particular he might be interested in going in Canada?" Michael asked

"No," Elizabeth said, "he talked about going to Canada like he thought it was a city."

The FBI and Michael made notes of that and would reach out to border patrol and local police and let them know this might be a possibility. Ethel went through some of the events that had impacted Arthur growing up.

"Arthur always loved and respected his brother, Frank, and avoided his dad as best he could. Frank Sr. and Frank Jr. went out of their way to make Arthur's life miserable, except those few times my husband took the boys hunting with him.

"Oddly, there were a few times he just took Arthur with him, like he was trying to bond with the boy. I always hoped those times went well, but nothing seemed to change after each weekend.

"His mental illness must be causing him to act this way, but I don't understand why he picked these young women as his victims."

"Young women would be easy targets for his rage," Sheila said.

"Arthur didn't have any friends growing up," Ethel said. "He got excited once when he thought a young girl was talking to him at school, but that ended pretty fast. There were a couple of guys Frank Jr. saw him talking to at school, but nothing after school. He never went to any school functions."

Ethel thought for a moment. "He got decent grades in school except for a couple of years in high school. That seemed to be when his mental issues began. I think that was about the time his dad took him on those weekend hunting trips. Also, he was never involved in any sports like Frank was. He was pudgier and not muscular at all."

Stephen was an FBI profiler who spoke up and said, "Arthur might be striking out at women as a way to kill his mother. We see this all too often. I'm not judging you, but he may feel like you should have done a better job of protecting him, so each time he kills, he's killing you, Mrs. Carol."

"That doesn't make sense," Ethel said, "because I did protect him. At times, I took a beating in his place. I gave him my love when no one else would. I'm the only woman he has ever loved."

Elizabeth quickly turned and looked at Ethel. "Did you have sex with Arthur?"

Ethel looked down at her hands. "I let him sleep with me a few times, when his father was away."

"You did, didn't you?" Elizabeth said. "Oh my God! He said a few times that you two were in love over the years!"

"It's not like you think!" Ethel said. "I had to help him. Who would love him if I didn't?"

"Did you have sex with Frank Jr. too?" Elizabeth asked.

"Of course not. He didn't need my love like Arthur did! Then, when he was older, he tried to protect me. His father was an evil man."

"Then why didn't you leave Frank Sr. when you had a chance?" Elizabeth asked.

"I thought about it," Ethel replied, "but didn't know where I'd go or what I'd do. I had no idea how I could raise those two boys on my own."

"Frank Jr. said Arthur was treated at a mental institution for a while," Michael said. "When and how did that happen, and how long did he stay there? It would be a good idea to reach out to that place and get information from them about Arthur's treatment and medication."

Ethel paused for a moment. "He started getting out of control toward the end of high school. He wasn't eighteen yet, and Frank Sr. found a place a short distance from our house that we could afford, but still in Pennsylvania, that he had Arthur committed to. I don't remember the name of it. Arthur stayed in there for three or four years, and they released him."

"Frank Jr. was in college then," Elizabeth said, "and that's where we met and dated. We got married right after graduation. I didn't meet Arthur until after we graduated and right before we got married."

The FBI agent asked Ethel how often they'd visited Arthur while he was in the mental institution.

"Frank went up there about once a month," Ethel said, "but I only went up there about once or twice a year. I guess that was bad of me, not seeing him more often than that, but I hated seeing him in there. He seemed so drugged and out of it."

The evidence was beginning to pile up and show that Arthur likely had some strong resentment toward Ethel.

Stephen spoke up and said, "Do you not see that you neglected him and caused a lot of his rage? You need to understand that."

When it ended, Michael spoke up and asked Ethel to find out the name of the mental institution Arthur had gone to and maybe who his doctor had been. Michael then told Ethel that she should allow the police or FBI to shelter her, too, until her son had been captured.

"Nonsense!" Ethel said. "My son would never hurt me. I refuse to be sheltered. If he does feel that way after all I've done for him, then maybe I deserve it, or maybe I could convince him to turn himself in."

Elizabeth smiled at Robert and Sheila in response to that comment. None of them thought Arthur would turn himself in.

Sheila approached Elizabeth, and they exchanged cell phone numbers, just in case the latter heard something that would help, or if she just needed someone to talk to. Elizabeth seemed very pleased to have Sheila's contact information. Ethel tried to grab Elizabeth's hand as they walked out of the station, toward the car, but Elizabeth wouldn't let her.

CHAPTER 19

SIXTH DEATH HOUSE

SHEILA AND ROBERT RETURNED TO THE HOTEL AND ONCE AGAIN ordered food in—neither of them felt like going to a restaurant to eat. They'd be driving to West Virginia the next day with police and FBI escorts. The house they needed to visit was an abandoned farmhouse.

The next morning, they ate, got ready to leave, and followed the police car. The Pennsylvania police car would meet a West Virginia state police car at the state line, and Robert and Sheila would follow the WV cruiser to the house. The FBI stayed a distance behind but had a device in Robert's Jeep to track them.

The FBI hoped that Arthur would start following Robert and Sheila, and they felt the same way. Robert didn't feel like it would be that easy, though. It was an hour-and-a-half drive to the farmhouse. It was a nice day, and Robert and Sheila really enjoyed the drive through the countryside in the Jeep.

Robert liked the country much better than the city. There were lots of trees and small hills along the way. They had to stop once at a Shell gas station to fuel up, and they got some snacks and a couple of drinks to hold them over until later.

Robert had been driving so far, but Sheila asked whether she could take a turn, and he had no problem with that. They followed the directions to the farmhouse.

Along the way, Sheila asked, "So do you regret taking this job?"

"Of course not," Robert replied. "I really wanted to help these families out, and felt that if they were right—and now we know they are—we needed to help catch the killer and make sure he stopped, one way or another.

"Also, I would never have met you if I hadn't taken this job, and that would have been sad."

She smiled. "I feel the same way. You really need to listen to me and be much more careful moving forward with this lunatic. You need to stay close to me."

"I promise I'll do a much better job," Robert said, "but lately, when I get in one of the visions, as you know, I'm not aware of what's going on around me."

"You're in danger, then, when you go there, and I need to make sure I focus on you and our surroundings."

They couldn't see the farmhouse from the main, single-lane road. They took the gravel driveway up to the house and parked. The police car followed them and came to a stop next to the Jeep. The officer saluted Robert and Sheila when they got out. They didn't see the FBI yet.

A beagle lay on the porch. Robert wondered why it was here.

"Do you think the owners left the dog behind?" Sheila asked.

He shrugged. "It seems to be comfortable here, though," he said, eyeing a nearby bowl of dog food and water.

Robert began sensing family feelings around the place. But it wasn't really robust—it was faint—so he assumed it must have been a while since those people had lived there. It was a typical farmhouse, painted white, with black trim, and a metal roof. At its rear stood a single tree, but another, felled tree lay by the front, having become firewood.

An old barn by the side of the house was in rough shape. Robert looked at the barn and felt a dark feeling drawing him there too. The death was supposed to have occurred in the house. He didn't feel like any children had been here for some time.

"Something's happened in the barn," Robert said. "We need to look there before we leave."

Sheila nodded.

This murder was supposed to have occurred recently. They went to the front door, and it was unlocked. The farmhouse appeared to be in solid condition. Old farmhouses out in the country like this one were rarely damaged by neighbors. The structures would age and fall apart, but seldom were windows busted out.

They walked inside, and Robert began hearing and feeling good and bad vibrations, like he normally did. The good vibrations felt weak—as though it had been a while. He looked around the first floor and saw nothing. The vibrations were happy on the first floor, which of course he liked. The only furniture they encountered was an old table in the kitchen and one chair. Robert hadn't gone into the vision yet. He told Sheila that they needed to go upstairs. She grabbed his hand and held it.

As they walked upstairs, the vision began creeping up on him. He stopped for a moment to immerse himself in it. The steps creaked as they continued onward. They turned, and there were three doors.

He pointed to the second door, and they walked toward it. From the room came a deep moan and then a thud. As they walked toward the threshold, light and dark flashed on the floor from what had to be shadows.

As they made the turn to enter the room, Arthur was standing over a woman lying on a piece of cardboard on the floor. Robert tightened his grip on Sheila's hand and stopped her. The woman was badly bruised already, and she seemed older than the other victims. This woman seemed to be in her midforties. She was thin and kind of rugged looking. He wondered for a moment whether she was a prostitute.

Arthur was cutting her clothes with a knife and tearing them off as she moaned and recoiled. She didn't seem as terrified as the previous young women he'd killed. Arthur pulled her up to her knees and pushed her face into his groin. He was unzipped and trying to assault her mouth.

She tried to please him, probably thinking he'd let her live. She moved back for a second and began laughing. She had one of those gravelly, longtime smoker voices.

"What's wrong, honey?" she said. "Can't you get it up for me?" She laughed again and went into a cough.

He pulled her back to his groin.

"Let Mommy try to help you," she said as reached up with her right hand to grab him.

He suddenly became enraged.

"You aren't my mother!" He grabbed her by the hair and lifted her to her feet.

"Take it easy, you son of a bitch! That hurts!"

He pulled a large butcher knife from the back of his pants, and she looked at it with large eyes as he shoved it through her stomach so hard the point came out her back. He removed it and pierced her all the way through her chest.

He threw her down on the cardboard then and kneeled over her. She looked up at him with surprise. She tried to ask him why as he resumed stabbing her over and over again.

Arthur was certainly losing it now. He was falling apart. He stabbed through her so hard the knife stuck in the hardwood floor under the cardboard. She seemed to be dead, but her mouth was still gasping and her eyes were open.

He stood up, threw his head back, and screamed as loud as he could. He moved over to the window and gazed out. He stood there for a few moments, took some deep breaths, and calmed down. He then turned and walked toward the door and out of the room. Robert examined the woman for any tattoos or scars he could write about. She had a couple of tattoos—a goldfish on her right forearm and a heart on the left side of her chest. She was still gasping, staring up at the ceiling.

"Something's wrong," Robert said.

He turned and went for the steps. He bounded down and out the front door, with Sheila right behind him. Outside, he saw Arthur enter the old barn. Robert ran toward the barn in his vision. He'd never done that before.

"What the hell is going on?" Sheila asked.

She ran in front of him with her gun drawn. She heard a car behind them start and drive toward the barn. She didn't look to see who it was yet. They walked into the barn slower, and Robert spotted Arthur. He'd tied up a younger brunette woman to a post.

Arthur walked toward her, and she looked frightened. He pulled out a smaller knife and cut the tape from the post. He slashed her a couple of times and walked her toward a nearby stall. He pushed her in, and she fell on the straw. Arthur began using the small knife on her. Then Robert began coming out of the vision—the woman in the house must have just died.

He turned and saw the FBI agents and the police officer watching and Sheila walking closer. He didn't say anything. He turned quickly and dived for the girl to uncover her. He pulled a bunch of the dirty old straw back, and there she was. She'd taken a piece of tape from her wrists and put it over her neck wound to staunch the bleeding.

Sheila ran forward and dropped down next to Robert. She reached for the girl and felt for a pulse. "She's still alive! We need to get her help as soon as possible."

The police officer and one FBI agent ran in, while the other called for help.

"Sheila," Agent Stephen said, "do you think she can be moved?"

Robert told them what Arthur had done to her, and they didn't say anything, but they all grabbed her gently and carried her out of the stall and into the daylight.

"They're going to fly a medevac here to get her," Agent Regina said.

Robert felt like he was in the way, so he walked to the porch of the house and sat down to decompress. The beagle walked over and lay next to him, and Robert began to pet the dog. His adrenaline was tanking now, and he was tired. Sheila was with the police, helping them with the girl for a bit. After a few minutes, the helicopter flew in and landed in the field in front of the house.

Agent Stephen said, "A neighbor found the deceased woman in the house recently, and the police responded to collect her."

The neighbor must have been the person feeding the dog. The woman in the house was the woman from West Virginia they'd been summoned to look at. She seemed to be a prostitute, so she must have been a convenient kill for Arthur. They didn't know yet how he'd picked up the young woman who'd barely survived, or who she was. The police hadn't discovered the young woman in the barn because they hadn't expected anyone else to be there and consequently hadn't searched well enough.

"That was amazing!" Sheila exclaimed as she approached Robert. "You saved another woman!"

She kissed him briefly on the lips and let him lay his head on her shoulder. The FBI agents came over, as well as a couple of WV police, and they were so thankful. Robert just nodded and chilled a bit. The sun was setting when things finally began to settle down. Robert had to run through his entire vision for the police and FBI before they left as there weren't any police stations close by that they could be taken to. Sheila told them they could call her and Robert the next day and they'd give them any more information they needed.

CHAPTER 20

SHEILA DECIDED TO DRIVE THE JEEP BACK. THEY FOLLOWED THE WV police to the border and the PA police to the hotel. They did see the FBI following them this time, but the agents still kept their distance. Sheila and Robert bought fast food again and took it to the hotel.

They started talking about moving back to Sheila's house. Some of these visions were far more difficult to overcome than others. Some of them rocked Robert to the core, and others didn't seem so bad—though they did seem to be getting worse. Robert skipped the following day before he began writing about this murder scene. They spent some time outside and went to see a movie. Sheila wanted them to go to her mother's house for dinner that evening. She said a couple of her brothers would be there too. Robert told her he'd like to do that.

Sheila wanted to stop and pick up a bottle of wine before they went to her mom's. Robert took one of his notebooks to begin drafting out his death journal about the West Virginia farmhouse. That would make it a little easier to pull together. They were both tired, but this visit would be good, and Robert was touched that Sheila wanted him to meet her family. He certainly hoped they liked him.

He'd already met her three police officer brothers at this point. Her mom, Sharon, greeted him with open arms, and he loved it. Her other two brothers and Jason were there for the dinner. Robert thought of *Blue Bloods* and how their family of cops and lawyers had dinner every episode. Sheila's mom made spaghetti and garlic bread. It was not an old homemade recipe. It was, however, delicious.

The conversation centered on their family and their dad for quite a bit, and then the Floreses began asking about Robert's family. They avoided discussing his paranormal gift. He knew they were curious about that, though, so eventually he rounded the corner and brought it up.

He explained about his family and their roots in Kentucky, and about his grandma's having the gift and how the car accident had made his own more active. They were all amazed, but no one acted afraid or awkward about it. He supposed being a family of cops had afforded them some bad and unusual situations too. Sheila spoke a while about some of the amazing things she'd witnessed with him.

"I was not a believer in this before," Sheila said, "but I am now."

Jason spoke up quickly, trying to get some recognition in this. "I told you, sis! I'm so glad you listened to me."

Sheila told them she was concerned because while Robert was in his vision, he could be prey to what might happen, and she intended to help him get through this.

With Sheila, Robert felt happier than he'd ever been before. She was quite a good person, and he hoped that someday he could introduce her to his family in Cincinnati. But the two of them needed to get past this situation first. He wondered whether it was wise to go back to her house and stay. He wasn't sure, but for some reason, it didn't seem much safer in the hotel.

He understood that the police didn't want to continue to watch her house every day and night. He wondered whether there was some way to draw Arthur out. How could they get him to expose himself to them? He would talk to Sheila and maybe Michael later. Sheila noticed that Robert was getting distracted and drifting off in thought, and she felt it might be time to head out.

She made an excuse for them to leave, and Robert told them each how delighted he was to meet them and that he hoped to see them again soon. They drove back to the hotel in his Jeep and discussed the positives and negatives of staying there any longer.

Arriving at the hotel, they were met with a fleet of police cars and a firetruck. Someone had set fire to Sheila's car and somehow broken into their room. As the police had run to the burning car, Arthur had invaded their room quickly. He'd just kicked the door in. They didn't find anything missing in the hotel room except for a couple of copies of Robert's latest death journal. Arthur was getting bolder.

Robert and Sheila grabbed their stuff from the hotel room and walked back down to his Jeep. Her car was a loss. They weren't quite sure what to do at this point. They decided to go to Sheila's house and wait until they figured out what to do. When they got to her home, one of the neighbors stopped over and talked to her.

He said everyone in the neighborhood was on edge about their being there. Sheila told him that she understood and that the two of them were trying to make a plan. Jason slept on the couch that night. There was a police car in front of the house all night, too, and probably one down the street.

The next two days, Robert worked on the death journal for the West Virginia farmhouse and barn. The young lady they'd saved in the barn had been from a nearby small town. She'd survived the attack and been left in the barn for four days. Her parents had contacted the police about her missing since she hadn't called them daily like she usually did. Arthur had snatched her off the street, just like he had Bethany—a victim of opportunity. They still didn't know much yet about the older woman who'd died in the house. Everyone thought she was probably an old hooker from a little larger town somewhere close by.

CHAPTER 21

ARTHUR HAD DECIDED HE NEEDED TO DO SOMETHING DRAMATIC TO leave his mark before he got caught or was killed. He was living in the woods in an old cabin that his dad had taken him and Frank to a few times when they were younger so that the two Franks could go hunting and have fun with young women from the area.

It'd been a little hard to find, but he'd finally located it. It was slightly west of their home, toward Ohio. He bought newspapers at night to try to stay up to date on what was going on. The old cabin had a TV, but it didn't work very well and received only one channel. He could tell that the cabin hadn't had any visitors for a long time.

Arthur didn't believe they knew which car he was driving since he always parked a good distance from each place. When he went to his old home, where he'd felt safe since everyone had left, he began parking on a road a short distance through the woods behind the house. He couldn't go back to the old family house for some time now if he wanted to avoid being caught.

They certainly know who killed those bitches now, Robert thought. This cabin would have to be his home for a while until he figured out someplace else. He started making plans for what he was going to do next. He wanted to do something to further hurt Frank—he needed to bring Larry here and groom him to be more like he was. He knew where Frank worked and had an idea about how to sabotage him. He had to be more careful now since anyone watching the news would recognize him.

Elizabeth had to decide what was best for Larry to be happy, safe, and healthy after they released Lexi's body and the family was able to put her to rest. Larry was fifteen and a little on the small side, but he was into sports and highly intelligent. She felt like leaving Frank was a good idea—they could move back to Maine, where her family was from.

She had a college degree in business and could stay with her family until she got a decent job and their own place to stay. She felt like once she divorced Frank, she would have some money from him, too, that would improve their conditions. Frank said he was a good businessman, and she knew he invested well. She could only hope that he wouldn't see this coming and try to figure out different ways to hide some of his money.

She knew Ethel would back her up, too, to try to help Larry. Larry had asked whether he could go out in the yard and fly a Frisbee and maybe hit some golf balls around. She didn't think there was any risk to either of them from Arthur, so she let him go. She figured the police should still be out there, too, as they'd said they would. Frank was at work and would probably come home late as usual, half-drunk from having been at his favorite bar. Ethel was somewhere in the house.

Frank had worked later than normal. His business was doing fairly well right now. The new secretary, Jasmin, wasn't like Wanda. She was a pretty young woman with a husband and a daughter. She had replaced Wanda when she had retired two years before, moving with her husband to Tampa, Florida.

Wanda had been with the company while Frank Sr. was there. Wanda was an attractive, shapely older woman with large breasts who every day wore a low-cut top and a skirt. She was very stern on how the office operated. One day, after his dad had passed away, Frank was in his own office, on the phone with a new client, when Wanda walked in with a notepad. She closed and locked the door, exposed her breasts, and then got on her knees and performed oral sex on him.

He was shocked and didn't know how to respond to her. He knew it was wrong to take part in this. She said she'd done it for his dad nearly every day for many years and might as well continue the tradition. It had become one of her duties. She cleaned up and left the room, like it was a part of her daily routine. She'd been true to her word until she'd left.

Frank was going to drop into his local bar and have a few drinks before he went home. He found his Mercedes in the parking lot, and before he got in, he noticed that someone had keyed the driver's side door. He got madder than hell.

I should just go back in and call the police and file a report, he thought. He then decided that would take too long, and he needed a drink, so maybe he could call the insurance company later—otherwise he couldn't stay out too long.

"What the hell!" he said. "I can take as long as I want. My dad would have done the same thing. Elizabeth will just have to get over it."

He got in, started the car, and drove away. He never noticed the trail of brake fluid he left behind in the parking lot. He looked around at the fading daylight and thought, *My poor Lexi. I will miss her the rest of my life*. He then thought about Larry. *I need to patch things up with him somehow and improve my relationship with Elizabeth. I should stop having sex on the side too. Dad said it was OK for a man to do, but I know it isn't.*

Frank started feeling bad for Larry and how he reminded him of Arthur. *I wish I knew where that scumbag was so I could get him put away.*

When Frank got to the second traffic light from his office, the car's brakes wouldn't work. He pumped and pumped them, but the car went right through the red light, and a van careened through the intersection and struck his passenger side.

Elizabeth was running around the house doing some cleaning and decided she should get something ready for supper. It would probably just be her, Ethel, and Larry again. She looked in the freezer and thought about making some meatloaf, mashed potatoes, and green beans. She located all the ingredients and put them on the kitchen counter in preparation.

Ethel walked into the kitchen, and they began talking about her ideas for dinner. Both decided the plan would be suitable for tonight.

"Do you think Frank will be home in time for dinner?" Ethel asked.

Elizabeth thought for a second. "He's probably working late again, and maybe later, since I told him I wanted to talk to him about Larry tonight."

"Or he's at the bar he and his father always liked."

They nodded.

Ethel remembered something. "Oh yeah—there was a car in the driveway a few minutes ago. What was that about?"

"I didn't know there was a car in the driveway. It's probably the FBI."

It was a nice, sunny day, so Robert and Sheila were out again close to Sheila's house, taking a walk on the trails. They'd been out for a while talking about anything but the murders and Arthur.

Suddenly Sheila asked, "Does that sound like sirens?"

Robert heard it then too. They both began jogging down the trail back to her house as the sirens grew louder. When they turned the corner and got on Sheila's street, there were three police cars in front of her house now.

When Robert and Sheila approached the house, Michael and Jason came out to meet them with grave looks on their faces.

"Good," Michael said, "you're both safe. Two bad things have happened that we need to let you know about. Let's go inside and talk."

They walked in the front door and shut the door behind them before Michael spoke again.

"It looks like someone cut the brake lines on Frank Carol's car," he said, "and he was involved in an accident. He's in the hospital getting some cuts and bruises looked at, but he'll live.

"The second problem is that Larry Carol has been abducted from his own driveway. We don't know for sure who did it, but we have a pretty good idea."

"I thought you have them being monitored by some of your officers," Sheila said.

"The officer who was there had a family emergency and had to leave right before the next shift was starting, so he didn't think it was a problem for him to leave ten minutes early. During that ten-minute window, someone got Larry out of his front yard."

"What the fuck!" Sheila said. "Someone should be there with them twenty-four hours a day until this is over!"

CHAPTER 22

THE HUNTING CABIN

ARTHUR THOUGHT THAT WAS MUCH EASIER THAN HE'D EXPECTED. He knew cutting Frank's brake lines would be simple as long as nobody saw him. Of course they'd know who did it. When he got to the house he wasn't sure if he'd be able to approach the house at all with the police watching them now. He'd hoped to kidnap any of the three at the house, either of the two women or Larry, but Larry had made that one easy too. *Now I can start grooming him*, Arthur thought.

He was also surprised that the officer at their house had driven off quickly, leaving no one else there to surveil. Arthur had just walked up behind Larry, who was wearing Lexi's headphones and never heard him coming. He grabbed the boy and taped his wrists and mouth shut, put him in the car, and left. He felt they could go back to the cabin and talk. *Larry will understand and be on my side*, Arthur thought. *We are the same. I just need to be persistent.*

Robert, Sheila, Jason, and Michael all went to the Carol house to understand what had happened and try to figure out where Arthur may have taken Larry. Everyone was upset. Even though Arthur had broken from his pattern with this latest kidnapping, it didn't mean he wouldn't harm the young man.

Robert was out of his element here. He didn't think there was anything he could do to help with this. He sat back and listened as Ethel and Elizabeth explained what had happened and answered questions. Ethel decided she would go to the hospital to be with Frank while Elizabeth stayed home in case Arthur reached out to her or they found him and returned him.

Sheila and Robert waited for a while, staying out of the way, until Michael told them they could go back to Sheila's until they figured out what to do. The FBI pulled up as Robert and Sheila were about to leave and said they needed to talk to Elizabeth and Ethel and then they'd meet up at Sheila's. As Robert drove them back in his Jeep, they talked and ran through the events, trying to understand what might have happened.

Larry wasn't very afraid of Uncle Arthur. Arthur had always been good to him, even though he was crazy. The way he dressed and acted was nasty, but Larry knew when to keep his mouth shut. He didn't believe Uncle Arthur would hurt him even though he'd kidnapped him. Arthur had always felt sorry for Larry since his dad treated him the same way Arthur had been treated by his own dad. Larry was sympathetic to Arthur's feelings too.

Uncle Arthur seemed to be pretty upset about everything that was going on, but he thought he'd heard someone say that Uncle Arthur had killed Lexi and more women. How could that be? He thought Arthur loved Lexi. Arthur always seemed mad at his dad for clearly favoring Lexi over him, but she was such a cool girl and was very popular at school, so he'd looked up to her too. When they arrived at this small cabin out in the woods, Uncle Arthur had taped him to a chair and said he would be right back.

Where did he go, and what is he going to do with me? Larry wondered.

He had listened and read how the man Robert Anderson had special abilities in the paranormal, and he thought that stuff was pretty cool. Larry knew he had some special abilities, too, that he'd used before.

Maybe I could send a mental message to Mr. Anderson and let him know where we are—if I knew exactly where I am.

He and Grandma Ethel would talk to each other occasionally with their minds. They were sitting on the couch one evening watching a game show when Larry suddenly heard *Larry can you hear me?* He wondered where that came from and as he looked about he saw his Grandma staring at him smiling. Suddenly he heard, *You can hear me can't you?* Her mouth didn't move. She suddenly pushed, *Try to think of something to tell me just in your thoughts. Think about just telling me.* He nodded his head and began trying to say things to his Grandma over and over and it didn't seem to be working. He suddenly looked intensely at her and said, *It's not working for me. I can't do it.* Then she mentally replied to him, *Yes you can. You just did it.* He laughed and realized he hadn't said that out loud and it did work. That was the beginning of many conversations that seemed to get stronger and better each time. He even sent his thoughts while he was at school and she replied to him. Just for fun, he was in math class one day and one of the cheerleaders was sitting across the room. He pushed to her, *Cheryl you are so pretty and have such pretty hair.* She began smiling and looking around as if she was looking for who might have said that. Then she appeared to be really confused about who might have said that. He wondered how this was possible and he did some research on the Internet which said something like this was fantasy and not possible. But he and Grandma continued to talk to each other without opening their mouths—she'd taught him how to push his thoughts to her, and she'd push back to him. Without saying a word, they'd made fun of his dad in the past when he was doing something dumb.

The FBI agents were outside Sheila's house now, keeping an eye on Sheila and Robert. Sheila wanted to do something to help, and she saw Robert pacing back and forth too. Michael said that Frank Carol was out of surgery and that he was going to be OK.

"Arthur is boxed in a corner now," Sheila said. "I'm glad that he isn't hurting or killing any more of these poor girls."

As far as they knew, he couldn't get out in public and continue his rampage. Anyone who saw him would recognize him and call the police. Michael told them there had been a few reports from people who thought they'd seen him that ended up being false. Sheila didn't think many people looked like him.

"I wish we could do something to help get the young Carol boy back."

She wondered why Arthur wanted the boy.

"Hey, Robert," she asked, "why don't we go to the hospital and talk to Frank and Ethel some more?"

"That's not a bad idea," Robert replied, "but I have a lot of visions in hospitals too. But I also just don't know how much longer I can sit around here doing nothing."

They went out to Robert's Jeep, got in, and drove by the FBI agents and told them what they wanted to do. The agents nodded their consent. The hospital wasn't too far away from Sheila's house. On the way, Robert reminded Sheila about her car and told her she needed to contact her insurance company, even though the circumstances would be hard to explain.

When they got to the hospital, they parked in the garage, got out, and started heading for the doors to the hospital. The FBI agents pulled up suddenly, said they had to go investigate a reported sighting of Arthur, and drove away.

"We'll be inside the hospital, "Robert said, "so we should be safe there."

Sheila nodded.

It was close to sunset, so the hospital was fairly quiet. They asked where Frank was and followed the directions to his assigned room. Ethel was sitting there half-asleep when they approached.

Hospitals were another sensitive place for Robert to go with his gift. People died at all hospitals, so he had various brief visions as he walked through. These messages or visions weren't violent deaths, so they weren't as strong as those he'd had of Arthur's murders. He would see faces and hear voices moaning and lots of crying and pain. This sort of vision had taken on a whole new perspective since he'd been drawn into these murder investigations.

As they passed Ethel, she sat up and said, "Frank is doing OK. He has a broken arm and some cuts and bruises, but he'll be OK. He seems to be humbled a little bit, which is good."

She asked whether there'd been anything new yet, and Sheila and Robert told her they had nothing to report.

"I know Arthur won't hurt Larry," Ethel said. "He won't do that."

"I hope you're right," Sheila replied. "He's in a desperate position right now."

Ethel knew Arthur better than anyone, though, so Robert and Sheila hoped she was right. They peeked into Frank's room, and he was asleep. His left arm was in a cast, and his face showed some scratches and bruises. They returned to the waiting room with Ethel and sat beside her.

As they sat there, faint thoughts—*hunting cabin*—began popping into Robert's head, and he wasn't sure why. *Why would I think* hunting cabin*?* he wondered.

After the third time, he said to Ethel and Sheila, "You know, I don't understand this, but I'm suddenly thinking *hunting cabin*."

Then came the thought, *I'm at a hunting cabin.*

"I'm at a hunting cabin," Robert said and looked at Ethel.

She smiled. "Larry's projecting those words to you. I told you that I have some powers too. Larry and I practiced this game for years when we were sitting around watching TV or playing cards with the family."

"Mental telepathy!" Sheila said. "Oh, what next?"

"Can you reply to him?" Ethel asked.

"I've never done that before," Robert said.

"I can project to him," Ethel said. "What do you want me to say?"

"Ask him if Arthur is there with him," Sheila said.

Ethel stared straight ahead for a few moments. "Nothing yet."

Larry sat there pushing his initial thoughts out to Robert, though he didn't know whether Robert was getting them. Suddenly he received, *this is Grandma. Are you all right?*

Oh, Grandma! Why didn't I think of that? I'm fine! Hungry. Arthur is gone.

How long has he been gone?

I don't know. I was asleep, but it's been a while.

Can you leave or escape?

No, I'm taped to a chair. I'll keep trying.

Arthur knew that Robert and his bitch would probably go to either his brother's house or the hospital. Robert should have stayed at his bitch's house with the FBI parked out front. He'd followed them to her house once, so he knew where she lived.

Arthur decided to go to the hospital and found a spot in the dark parking garage where he could see arriving vehicles. Then he waited. Robert and Sheila pulled a Jeep into the garage and parked, and as they walked toward the hospital entrance, the FBI for some reason drove away.

How lucky can I get? Arthur thought. *I guess this was meant to happen. The cops and FBI just keep leaving the people they're supposed to be protecting.*

Now was his chance to do something to hurt Robert. It was another long shot that one of them might come outside alone, but going inside the hospital was too risky. He would just hide and wait by the garage in the dark. Things had been going his way so far, so he hoped the streak might continue.

Ethel had stopped receiving messages from Larry, and Robert hadn't received any more since Larry had started talking to his grandma. Ethel sat trying to explain how Robert could send a telepathic message to her, but so far, he'd had no success. Robert even tried to send a message to Sheila, with no luck. This would be a new type of skill or ability he could use when he figured it out—if he could. They sat for a while, and Robert asked Ethel whether she remembered where the hunting cabins were that they'd used.

"There were two they stayed in," she said, "but I never knew where they were."

She remembered that at first Arthur would feel good after returning from those trips because he felt like one of the guys. However, he'd never been allowed to actually go hunting. Frank Jr. had actually taught Arthur how to shoot a rifle, a shotgun, and a pistol because it was fun.

Robert asked her to think long and hard or even call someone who might help her remember where the cabins were. When Frank woke up, they could ask him. He would surely remember those details. As they waited, they began to get hungry. The cafeteria was closed now, so they couldn't get anything to eat except from a snack machine. Robert found a couple of machines and brought back some coffee, chips, and nuts. Ethel was fine with eating the chips.

"I'm not going to eat that crap!" Sheila said. "That stuff is so bad for you, and who knows how long they've been in there. I want a burger and some fries!"

"Well," Ethel said, "I don't think that's much better for you."

"OK," Robert said. "Let's go get some food and bring it back and eat with Ethel here. Frank should be waking up soon, and we can find out what he knows about the hunting cabins."

"I think it's best for me to go," Sheila said, "and for you to wait here. I won't be long, and he could wake up anytime."

Robert didn't want Sheila to go alone. It was so risky right now since Arthur was still on the loose, but they did need some protein, and Ethel hadn't eaten in hours either. He might even be able to learn more about telepathy while Sheila was gone.

"OK," Robert said. "And the FBI should be out there again anyway. Be very careful, keep your phone close and don't take too long."

Sheila got up and hugged Robert. "I'll be fine!" she said and headed for the door.

Robert watched her round the corner for the elevator and thought, *Man, I'm crazy about her. God, please don't let anything happen to her.* He sat back down and waited.

The atmosphere of the hospital tonight was no different from that of any other evening. The nurse's station was a short distance down the hall. At times there were up to four nurses sitting there and at other times just one. They had monitors around, Robert assumed, to watch higher-risk patients in their rooms.

They would walk back and forth in what seemed like a random fashion, but he knew they were doing their jobs checking up on patients. Occasionally someone with the cleaning crew would be pushing a cart up and down the halls. They stopped a couple of times and asked them whether they needed anything.

Sheila went to the first floor, which was vacant at this time of day. It was dark outside now, so she walked to the revolving door, which wouldn't turn after hours. She went to the other door, pushed it open, and went outside.

She paused for a moment to take in the evening atmosphere. She hated hospitals. They were always so gloomy and solemn. She couldn't imagine how difficult a place like this was for Robert. Suddenly she thought, *It would be nice to smoke a cigarette at a moment like this*, but she'd made the smart decision to stop a couple of years ago.

She stretched her arms up over her head and wondered what the best nearby restaurant was. She turned and started heading for the garage to find the Jeep, and as she rounded the corner into the dark garage, she felt a sudden pain in the back of her head.

Arthur still couldn't believe his luck. It seemed like with every step he took, he was presented with an extraordinary opportunity. This was meant to be. He was a very patient man, and he waited in the darkness for a while when suddenly Robert's bitch walked out the front door of the hospital, with the FBI still nowhere in sight. He waited for Robert to walk out behind her, but it never happened. He wanted Robert.

She turned and was clearly not looking around for him, and that was a big mistake. She walked slowly his way, and he thought, *she's going to be fun.* Maybe he could even get an erection with her. He was going to take her back to the cabin and make Larry watch, like Dad made me watch, and maybe he'd help him kill her. How great that would be—to see how much that would hurt Robert, and for Larry to be one step closer to being like him.

After he struck Sheila in the back of the head with the hammer, Arthur caught her before she could fall to the concrete and carried her to his car. He sat her in the passenger seat, taped her hands and feet together, and wound a piece of tape around her head, covering her mouth. He looked around and saw a couple of nurses in the distance talking, but he didn't think they saw him, or else they'd have been acting much differently.

He backed out of his spot and accidentally squealed his tires a little as he pulled away. He looked over at Sheila, and she was out. She had a pretty face, and he couldn't wait to kiss and lick all over it like he'd done with the other women. The mere thought of it aroused him.

He smiled. "We're going to the cabin to have some fun with Larry and teach him a few things!"

The two nurses noticed something off about the big guy getting in his car. He seemed to be doing something to the passenger. He stopped and looked over at them, and they acted like they were having a casual discussion about something until he got in his car and hightailed it out of the garage.

They tried to get the license plate number but caught only two letters: *OW*. The car was some sort of dark-colored Ford sedan. They ran into the hospital to report that something had just happened in the garage, first telling security and then calling the police.

CHAPTER 23

HE HAS HER

ROBERT'S CELL PHONE SUDDENLY BEGAN VIBRATING. HE THOUGHT IT might be Sheila calling, but it was Michael.

He answered the phone, and Michael suddenly asked, "Where is Sheila?"

"She decided to go out for some food and should be back soon."

"Shit!" Michael said. "Sorry—I don't think so. Two nurses reported an incident in the parking garage a few minutes ago. They saw a large dark man doing something to a passenger in his car before driving off. He pulled out and left in a hurry. I think Arthur may have Sheila."

A few minutes later, Sheila woke up slowly and quietly. The back of her head hurt a lot. She realized she was in the passenger seat of a moving vehicle, with her hands and her feet bound and her mouth taped shut. The car smelled something awful. In her peripheral vision, she saw who she knew was Arthur Carol. What a huge ugly guy he was.

She decided to remain quiet and watch for landmarks to understand where they were going. She watched the clock on his dash to try to figure out how far he was taking her. He was driving slow so that he didn't attract any police attention. They drove along for quite some time across the dark countryside, and Sheila at times felt his eyes on her.

"I know you're awake," he said.

She didn't answer. Suddenly her phone began vibrating in her pocket. But she didn't move. She thought that what she did at this point was her life or death and maybe she could save the boy, Larry, too. She knew that they were already beginning a plan to look for her. She knew her brothers would be all over this and find her fairly soon. Was there anything she could do to help them? Then she remembered that maybe Larry could talk to his grandma telepathically, and she knew that would help to let them know where they were.

Robert got off the phone and told Ethel what had happened. A nurse walked by at that moment and went into Frank's room.

"Mr. Carol, it's time to wake up and let me check your vitals."

She turned the light on, and Frank winked awake, blinded by the ceiling lights.

"I know I was in a car wreck," Frank said. "Tell me the bad news."

The nurse told him that he had a broken arm and had sustained other cuts and bruises but that it wasn't a horrible accident. They had already put a cast on his arm.

"Your mother and a friend are in the hallway," she said when she finished with his tests. "Your blood pressure is fine, and your pulse is strong."

She felt around on his arms and legs and asked whether he sensed her touch.

"Yes," he replied, "that's all fine."

Ethel and Robert entered the room and began to let Frank know what had happened.

"Arthur caused your wreck by cutting your brake lines," Robert said. "He kidnapped Larry and has him someplace and just recently kidnapped Ms. Flores.

Do you have any idea where the cabins are that you, your dad, and Arthur stayed in on hunting trips?"

Ethel nodded, walked over, and held Frank's hand. "Remember you guys went to a couple of cabins in the woods to hunt occasionally?"

Frank nodded. “Arthur has Larry and Ms. Flores now?”

“Yes, he’s had Larry for a few hours, taped up in a cabin where you guys used to go, and about thirty or forty minutes ago, Arthur grabbed Sheila from the garage here too.”

Suddenly Jason and Michael walked into the room out of breath.

“We have to know where your killer brother’s taken our sister,” Michael said.

“I remember two cabins that we used to go to,” Frank said. “I don’t remember exactly where they’re at, but I’m sure I can find them. We have to save them and stop that bastard!”

“Wait, you aren’t going anywhere, Mr. Carol. You were just in a car wreck, and you need to recover before you’re allowed to leave.”

“Two people’s lives are at stake here, Nurse. We need to do whatever we can to save them.”

Frank jerked the IV out of his arm and turned to get out of bed. Robert went over and helped him up to his feet.

Michael looked at the nurse. “Please get his clothes so he can get dressed.”

The men all left the room while Ethel and the nurse helped Frank get dressed to leave. There were several more police officers here now waiting to understand what they needed to do. Jason found a room close by so they could talk and develop a plan. They all went into the room, and someone produced a map of the area that they could look at. Frank had a general idea where both cabins were, but they needed to somehow narrow it down further.

Sheila squinted to read the street signs. They’d gone off the paved roads finally and were on gravel roads, which she felt was going to put them closer to a cabin. The last turn he took was onto Raccoon Road. She needed to remember that. Arthur asked her whether she was awake, and she didn’t reply. He backhanded her thigh and repeated the question, but she remained silent.

“Well, I guess I hit you in the right spot, or harder than I thought,” Arthur said. “Gosh, I hope you didn’t die. Where’s the fun in that?”

She kept quiet and let her head bounce as the car traveled up the long driveway.

He stopped in front of a small cabin, got out, and went around to her side. Then he opened the door and pulled her out. She'd decided to wait until she laid eyes on Larry before she fought back. He picked her up, placed her across his right shoulder, and carried her into the cabin.

He tossed her on a couch, and now Sheila could see Larry. He was taped to a chair across the room. There was a fire going in a small fireplace and a couple of lamps turned on, but it was still fairly dark. Before Arthur did anything else, he walked over and reached into Sheila's pocket suddenly and yanked her cell phone out. Sheila didn't have a good angle, or she would have kicked him in the head or in the balls.

Arthur didn't believe she was still unconscious. He thought she was faking. He was prepared for her to fight back, or so he thought.

He kneeled down in front of Sheila. "You see, Larry, this is what you do with these bitches. That's what your grandpa used to say when we were here. I saw him have sex with a few whores when we spent time in these cabins. This is where your grandpa taught me how to deal with these bitches. This is where your dad got started with women."

Arthur reached over and grabbed Sheila by her right breast through her shirt and squeezed.

Sheila opened her eyes and looked directly into Arthur's with rage.

"There she is," he said.

At that moment, Sheila leaned forward and slammed her right elbow hard into Arthur's nose, breaking it. She knew she had little time to react as he fell backward screaming. She saw him drop a small knife, and she grabbed it and cut the tape from her hands, then pulled it from her mouth.

She looked at Larry. "Tell Grandma Raccoon Road."

He nodded. He knew what she wanted him to do.

She reached down to cut the tape off her ankles, and Arthur grabbed her wrist. He was a very strong man. He wrenched her wrist, hurting her, and threw her back to the couch. He began to stand, and she started to go at him again.

He took a swing at her head with his right hand, and she ducked. He immediately followed it with a left uppercut, and she couldn't move in time. He caught her squarely under the chin and knocked her backward to the couch. She was stunned, but she'd been hit harder when she'd studied self-defense in the military and martial arts after that.

Larry went into his little zone. *Grandma, are you there?*

Ethel suddenly pulled back. "Larry's reached out to me again."

Yes, I am, Larry.

The lady just got here, and she told me to tell you Raccoon Road.

Ethel turned to Robert and Frank. "Sheila's there at the cabin with Larry, and she told him to relay *Raccoon Road*."

The police officers looked at one another wondering what the hell was going on.

Frank thought for a moment. "Oh yeah—that's where one of the cabins is located. It's on Raccoon Road!"

It was a small gravel road that wasn't even on the map, but Frank pointed to where the cabin was.

"Let's go!" Michael said. "Frank, ride with me. Mrs. Carol and Robert, ride with Jason. He said lights and sirens."

As they were running for the front door, he added, "We'll call ahead and tell any police closer to the location to get their asses over there immediately!"

They all climbed in the police cars and sped off. At first, there were about five or six cars in their group, and it expanded as they went.

Robert could hear Michael on the speaker telling the police ahead of them to get any cars out of the way so that they could fly to Raccoon Road. Robert thought this was the fastest he'd ever traveled by car in his life. Michael called for an ambulance to meet them at the scene, too, just in case. From the back seat, Robert silently prayed to God that Sheila and Larry would be OK. Ethel grabbed his hand, held it tightly and prayed with him

Sheila was not going to go down easily. She yanked the tape off her ankles and jumped back up behind the couch in a fighting stance.

Arthur picked up a towel and wiped his nose to clear off the blood and tears. Then he grabbed his nose and cranked it to straighten it out a bit before wiping some more.

He began walking to the left of the couch, and Sheila walked in the opposite direction, trying to keep the couch between them.

When she got around to Larry, she slyly reached behind her and handed Larry the small knife she'd used to cut her tape.

Larry held it down and slowly, unobtrusively, started cutting his hands free.

Arthur walked to the right, and so did Sheila. He stepped over the back of the couch to try to close the distance, and Sheila used a Muay Thai kick and slammed her shin into his. He yelled and pulled it back.

He thought for a minute and tried it again, and when she kicked him, he almost grabbed her foot.

He growled loudly, reached for the couch, and just threw it out of the way before moving toward her. She went to elbow him in the head, but he was undeterred, continuing his advance. She sidestepped to the left, and he grabbed her, dragging her down with him as he fell to the floor.

He struggled trying to get on top of her as she slid to her side on the rough hardwood floor.

"You really stink," she said, "and you're going to die soon. Did you know that?"

He laughed. "We'll see."

"Your brother survived the wreck and told them where we are."

"He doesn't remember where this cabin is," Arthur said. "We haven't been here for a long time."

Sheila glanced at Larry, who'd cut the tape all loose, and softly enunciated the word "Run."

Larry shook his head and walked over, pulled back, and kicked his uncle Arthur in the head as hard as he could.

Arthur looked around at him. "What the hell are you doing? You're like me. I'm going to teach you how to take care of these bitches just like your grandpa taught me!"

Arthur raised up and managed to bring a hard punch down and land it on Sheila's head. She was dazed for a moment, and he took advantage of the situation, climbing on top of her.

Larry tried to aim and take another kick at Arthur, but Arthur deflected it with his left forearm and then pushed Larry back against the wall.

The cabin was out in the middle of nowhere, and no police officers were very close to it. The closest was about ten minutes away, but he kicked it into high gear. The young cop, Tim, knew the area pretty well and thought he remembered where the cabin was.

He wished he had an SUV instead of a cruiser since the gravel roads weren't in great shape. Tim had been on the force for only three years. Into the radio he yelled, "This is officer Tim Ransom, and I can be at the cabin in about ten minutes." He looked at the shotgun next to him and thought that would be the right weapon for this.

Arthur had Sheila now. He grabbed her wrists in his left hand and began tearing her top off with his right.

Larry yelled at him to stop.

"Is this how you treated Lexi?" Larry said. "Why are you so evil? You killed my sister! I'll never get to see her again! I hope she's right and you do die soon, Uncle Arthur!"

Arthur stopped for a moment and looked at Sheila. He turned to Larry and was almost regretful in that moment. Then he growled loudly and punched Sheila two more times in the head, knocking her out.

Larry looked around the room and got the fireplace poker, and as Arthur began trying to pull Sheila's pants and bra off, Larry hit him hard in the back of the head.

Arthur fell to the floor, stunned for a moment. Then he began to cry softly. "You don't understand. We're the same!" He stood and headed toward Larry. He grabbed the sledgehammer off the nearby table and eyed it before meeting Larry's gaze.

Sheila awoke and saw what was going on. "Run, Larry! Get out of here. You need to get away! You can't beat him!"

Arthur spun around with the hammer and looked at Sheila, and suddenly Larry ran for the door, opened it, bounded down the porch steps, and disappeared in the dark. Arthur growled loudly and began following him, and when he reached the small porch, he heard a distant police siren. Then he saw blue light filtering through the trees.

At the threshold, he turned to Sheila. "Tell them I'm not done yet. You're another lucky bitch! Oh yeah, tell them there's a cemetery out back. Frank doesn't even know that. Dad made me help bury them."

He turned and headed off in the direction opposite the one Larry had taken.

As Tim pulled up to the cabin, he saw a young guy running away and knew that wasn't the killer. Then he saw Arthur moving off in another direction.

He picked up his radio. "This is unit 1024, and I'm 10-97. I saw a young man and the killer running away from the cabin."

After parking the cruiser, he removed the shotgun from the rack and got out.

Tim looked around in circles to try to see where Arthur was and to make sure he was safe to approach the cabin. Stepping to the door, he had the shotgun leveled but his finger away from the trigger. He looked in the door and saw a naked woman trying to hide herself, and as he began to speak to her, she looked frightened for a moment and pointed a finger.

Arthur stepped up and hit Tim really hard in the back of the head with the hammer. Tim fell to the floor and accidentally discharged the shotgun, hitting some buckshot into Sheila's left leg.

Arthur ran down, jumped in the cruiser, turned the lights off, and drove away. Fifteen minutes after Arthur drove off in the cruiser, other police cars began arriving. Because Arthur had taken Sheila's cell phone and the police car was gone, she hadn't had any way to reach anyone, so she'd decided to just sit and wait.

She straightened up her clothes, stepped out onto the porch, and yelled outside for Larry, but he never responded. She hoped Arthur hadn't picked Larry up as he left. Officers stormed the cabin and began looking all around the area but were careful to preserve the scene.

An ambulance had arrived on the scene, too, once the police said it was OK. One of the EMTs dressed her wounds but insisted she go to the closest hospital to remove the buckshot. This was the first time Sheila had been shot, and she hoped it was the last.

Sheila had checked the police officer and thought he was dead. He was a young guy. That was so sad. The EMTs had confirmed he was dead, too, but left him there until forensics came. One of the police officers had brought Sheila a small blanket to cover up with since her blouse had been ripped off. She had ice and was holding it to her head. Suddenly Michael and Jason came into the cabin. They ran to her and hugged her.

"Where's Robert?" she asked.

They looked around, and Michael said, "He was right behind us. That's odd."

As Robert approached the porch, he began feeling some bad vibrations. He was surprised and didn't understand. He could tell there had been deaths here and they weren't recent. He wanted to get inside and see Sheila, but he was drawn into a vision. He saw a pretty young black woman walking up the steps with a man who looked like Frank Sr.

She was laughing and having a good time and seemed pretty drunk. Frank Sr. looked drunk too. Robert suddenly saw a twelve- or thirteen-year-old Arthur walking up, too, following them in. Then Robert saw a separate incident, like an echo of the first, with a glimpse of Frank Sr. with a pretty, young red-haired woman.

The furniture looked nice for an old hunting cabin. This was like Arthur's room at the old Carol house. If Robert was seeing this, the girls must have died here. Frank Sr. led the young Black woman into the cabin and back toward the single bedroom, where he began roughly undressing her.

"Hey," she said, "take it easy, man!"

Frank Sr. slapped her on the face. "Shut up, bitch."

He finished undressing her and pulled his pants down. He penetrated her and began having sex with her aggressively and making Arthur watch. Frank clutched the woman's hands in his left so she couldn't fight back.

Robert heard both women groaning and yelping while Frank assaulted them. He saw glimpses of Frank Sr. doing the same thing with the young redheaded woman. He felt there were other victims, too, but didn't see them.

Arthur sat on a chair in the bedroom trying not to look at first, but the sensations overtook him. As his father continued sexually assaulting the woman, Arthur began to watch much more closely.

Robert saw both women looking up at Frank Sr. after he'd used them. Then Frank Sr. slowly began holding one, then the other, around her throat, using his weight to choke her. Each woman tried to pry his hands off, with no luck. Frank Sr. laughed at the women while they struggled to breathe.

It took a few minutes for Frank to choke them until they were dead. After the Black girl stopped moving, he began touching her body all over.

"Come over here, boy, and feel this bitch's tits and pussy!"

Arthur timidly walked over, and his dad grabbed his hands and held them where he wanted Arthur to touch her.

After Frank Sr. seemed satisfied, he picked up the body and said, "Come on, boy—we need to get rid of her."

Frank carried her out the door.

Then Robert saw the echo of Frank carrying the young redhead out the door.

"Now you're part of this," Frank said, "helping your old man."

He said, "You're just like me."

Sheila registered that Robert was in a vision and told the officers to leave him alone while he went through it. When Robert came out of the vision, he was inside the cabin in the bedroom. Several first responders were standing around him. He was shocked and looked at each of them in turn.

"This is a death house too," Robert said. "Frank Sr. killed at least two young women here and made Arthur watch, participate, and help get rid of them."

Everyone was quiet for a few moments.

"Before he left," Sheila said, "Arthur said Frank Sr. used to come here to hunt, but he brought young hookers here to have sex too. He said this is where Frank Jr. lost his virginity. The last thing Arthur said when he left was that there are bodies buried behind the cabin. I think Larry got away—he may be safe outside somewhere."

Suddenly Larry walked inside with a police officer. He had been hiding, as he should have been. Ethel and Frank didn't come inside until Larry showed up.

Sheila told them both, "Larry was very brave trying to fight his uncle Arthur, and I know he saved my life."

"Thank you, lady," Larry said.

Ethel and Frank both got close to Larry and tried to comfort him.

CHAPTER 24

ARTHUR KNEW HE COULDN'T DRIVE THE POLICE CAR FOR LONG. HE'D tossed the bitch's cell phone out the window after leaving the cabin. It was an older police car, so it probably didn't have a GPS tracker. He would look for a parking place to hide—as well as another car. He really wanted to kill that Robert Anderson's bitch and let Larry watch. Then he wanted to kill Robert.

He spotted an old abandoned factory right off the road, so he pulled in and around the back of the building to conceal the police car, coming to a stop behind an old dumpster. He decided he'd go inside the factory for a bit and rest before he figured out what to do next.

He was tired, and Robert's bitch and his own nephew had hurt him and fought harder than he'd expected. He'd thought Larry would understand what he was doing and want to help him. He found a door to the factory that looked weak and forced it open easily. He didn't think there would be an alarm. It looked like it had been out of use for a long time. He found some cardboard piled up and put it out of view of any window and lay down to rest. He could hear mice or rats running around in the distance.

Sheila and Robert went to the hospital to get her shotgun wounds cleaned up. The shot fortunately had gone mostly beside her, and she'd received only a few pellets in her shin. Once she'd been tended to, a police officer drove them to Sheila's house. In the back seat, Sheila leaned against Robert and fell asleep.

She'd had a traumatic day and was seriously sore from Arthur's assault and the shot in the leg. Robert felt good returning the emotional support and comfort for once. Once they arrived at the house, Robert helped Sheila to bed and lay down with her too.

"I'm so tired and sore," she said.

"I would think so," Robert said. "You had a bad day, and I knew I should have gone for that food."

"That's nonsense! I could probably fight him better."

He didn't think he was tired, but he went right off to sleep too. He'd seen a police car pull up when they'd arrived, so he felt safe, even though Jason hadn't been there to spend the night again. During the night, Sheila moaned from time to time, probably from the pain.

Frank Jr., Ethel, and Larry were taken back home too. Elizabeth was so excited to see her son. Frank seemed to be trying to figure out how to get closer to Larry.

"I need to take you out soon," Frank said, "and teach you how to handle guns and shoot."

Larry looked deeply into Frank's eyes and said, "Thanks, Dad! I'd love to learn how to shoot a pistol and a shotgun."

They'd all gone through a traumatic day. They sat down with Elizabeth and explained what had happened. She was shocked at how bold Arthur had become.

"Do you think there's a police car out front still?" Elizabeth asked.

"We saw one parked out front when we pulled in," Frank replied.

"Do you think they'll stay there? They've been leaving, and somehow that's when he strikes!"

The next morning, the FBI came to check on them and make sure they were OK. They said they would be watching them, too, as much as they could, until they caught Arthur.

Frank was still clearly in some pain. Larry was happy because of what he'd done to help Sheila, but he was still nervous about his uncle. He was sure he'd completely enraged Uncle Arthur. He knew Uncle

Arthur didn't understand why he didn't just do what he expected him to do.

I'm not a killer! Larry thought. *What happened to him to make him that mean? He killed my sister!* He would find out eventually.

They were all still very shocked about everything that had happened over the last few days. Lexi had been killed cruelly by Arthur. The police should release Lexi's body to them soon so they could give her a proper burial. Frank wondered what had made Lexi a target for Arthur's rage. What was he thinking? He'd seen Lexi grow up. What had suddenly triggered his rage?

Before the rest of the family retired to bed, Frank talked to Elizabeth and Ethel about maybe leaving for a while to avoid being someplace where Arthur could easily find them.

"I'll stay up and alert the rest of the night," Frank said, "to try to prevent Arthur from attacking us. In the morning, I'd like to discuss a place, or places, we might go to stay away from him until he's captured. If you're OK with that."

None of them thought Arthur was smart enough to dodge law enforcement for long. They clearly didn't understand him at the moment. He would be a victim of his desires. They all certainly hoped that he didn't kill anyone else.

Frank thought, *That damned doctor who released him from the mental hospital should be held responsible too. He should have never let Arthur out.*

Frank made some coffee and planned to watch TV or read to stay awake until the morning.

Arthur woke in the early morning. He needed to wait until dark to visit his family. He left the factory, and the old police cruiser, and went looking for another car. He came upon a neighborhood a couple of miles away and began checking car doors as he walked along.

He found an old dark Dodge van sitting on the street close to some houses, but a little distance away, by some trees. He checked the front doors, and they were locked. He tugged the handle of the rear door, and it yielded. He climbed in the van, went up to the driver's seat, and began to look around. He found the key in the ashtray and smiled. He sat in the driver's seat, and the van rumbled to a start. Not seeing anyone out looking, he drove off. He still had some money in his jacket pocket, but he'd left most of it in his car, which was now in police custody.

Frank managed to stay awake most of the night. In the morning, when the women were up and drinking their coffee, he told them he'd been on the internet.

"I found some places we might want to go to be safe," he said. "So maybe we can go someplace warm like the Bahamas or Miami, or we could go to someplace like Denver or even England. If there's any other place, let's talk about it."

Arthur drove toward his brother's house first. He had to stop and fuel up at a busy gas station. He filled the tank and headed for the pay window. He didn't have a credit card, so he would pay with cash. Credit cards were too easy to trace anyway. He made sure the hood of his jacket was pulled up to obscure his face as he paid, though the guy taking the cash didn't even look up at him.

After Arthur left, he drove into a large Walmart parking lot, zeroed in on a car hidden behind some bushes, and stole the license plate for the van. He always had on him a Swiss Army knife with a screwdriver accessory. He then continued on closer to his brother's house. He knew there would be police there and maybe FBI this time.

When Arthur approached the house, he decided to park in the woods a distance from the house, where he would wait until it was nearly dark out. In this part of the country, it got dark earlier in the fall. Tonight was a new moon, so there would be no moonlight, which was perfect. The van was well hidden where it was parked. It would allow him to possibly sneak up on the police car.

When it started getting dark, he had to walk for a few minutes through the woods to get close to the house. It was so dark out that he tripped over some downed branches, but fortunately, he'd always been blessed with the ability to see pretty well in the dark. He waited until it was about midnight to approach the police car.

Finally he saw the police car and heard the officer's radio blaring. The driver's window was down, and Arthur could see the cop sitting there with his eyes closed. He slowly approached the police car and hid behind a tree and some bushes. He had his hammer and a knife and was ready for his next steps.

The cop would have a gun, though, so Arthur would have to be stealthy to sneak up on him. He knelt down and picked up some rocks from the roadside. He threw the first rock to makes noises to attract the cop. The officer opened his eyes and looked around. Arthur waited a couple of minutes and threw the second rock. The cop turned on a flashlight and shined it in the direction Arthur had thrown the rock.

Since the cop didn't see anything, he shined the light around the entire area. From where he was crouched, Arthur knew he wouldn't be exposed. He also knew that turning the flashlight on would make the police officer a little blind; his eyes would have to readjust to the dark.

Arthur threw another rock.

The cop picked up his mic. "10-96, I'm getting out of the car to check out some noises."

"10-4—be careful!"

He got out of the cruiser, and he must have left the key in the ignition, since the car began the *ding-ding* sound that indicated as much. He turned the flashlight on again, drew his handgun, and walked toward where the noise was coming from.

Arthur was still hiding behind a tree. When the cop got closer, Arthur threw another rock, and the cop turned his back to Arthur and toward the noise. Arthur slowly crept toward the cop, but a twig broke underfoot. The cop turned as Arthur charged him. The cop got one shot off and missed before Arthur hit him with the hammer.

The cop didn't even have time to raise his arms to defend himself. As the cop fell to the ground, he got off a second shot and hit Arthur in left shoulder.

Arthur held the cop down, sat on him, and hit him with the hammer until he stopped moving. Arthur reached down and took the cop's gun.

The gunshot hurt like hell, but he was on a mission. He might die tonight, but not without hurting, or hopefully killing, others.

Arthur knew his family in the house had to have heard the gunshots. He climbed into the police car and turned off the police radio. He waited for a few minutes and then began to drive slowly toward the house.

Inside the house, the family heard the gunshots, and Frank told them he'd go and check it out. None of them had had a chance to go to sleep yet. Ethel and Larry didn't speak, but they both sent telepathic messages to Robert, telling him they'd heard gunshots and thought Arthur was there.

Robert heard them both and immediately jumped up off the couch and turned to Sheila. "Arthur's at the Carols' house! Ethel and Larry both just sent me a message!"

Suddenly, Sheila got a text message from Elizabeth, then a call.

"Help us!" Elizabeth said. "He's here!"

"You must hide!" Sheila said.

Elizabeth then put the phone in her pocket. Sheila could still hear them talking in the background.

She and Robert didn't have to say anything as they ran for the door and out toward the police car, where Jason now was.

"Arthur's at the Carols' house!" Sheila yelled. "We need to get there as fast as we can!"

Jason said, "Jump in!" and they did while he screamed down the street again.

CHAPTER 25

ARTHUR SLOWLY DROVE THE POLICE CAR TOWARDS THE HOUSE. THE lights and siren were off. Frank exited the house when he saw the police car slowly driving up toward house and yelled to the family, "I'm going outside to talk to the cop to see what's going on." Frank stepped outside and waited.

The police car pulled up and stopped a short distance away. Frank wondered why the car had stopped so far away and decided to walk over to the cruiser to find out what was going on. Suddenly, Arthur stepped out of the vehicle.

"What the hell are you doing and why are you here?" Frank said.

Arthur raised the gun and shot Frank twice before the gun jammed. Frank moaned loudly before falling to the ground and lying motionless. Arthur threw the gun down, walked over to Frank's body, and nudged him with his foot before he turned towards the house. Frank didn't make any sound or movement. The gun had served its purpose but wasn't as much fun as using the hammer and a knife.

Arthur had wanted to kill Frank Jr. all along, but if by some miracle Frank lived he would have to suffer knowing what Arthur did tonight, in addition to his killing Lexi. Arthur went to the front door and peeked inside but didn't see anyone.

Ethel, Elizabeth, and Larry had heard the two additional gunshots right outside the house.

"Oh my God," Elizabeth said, "that can't be good". She yelled, "Frank! Frank!"

She shifted her focus to protecting her son and mother-in-law.

"Let's go to Frank's office."

She remembered Frank had a gun safe there. They entered the room, and she walked to the safe. She also knew that Sheila would be able to hear anything else she said. She tried to enter three different combinations into the safe, but it wouldn't unlock.

She turned to Larry. "Do you know what the combination is?"

"Dad never gave me that," Larry said.

She looked at Ethel.

Ethel shook her head. "I don't know it either."

Elizabeth looked around and grabbed one of Frank's precious baseball bats.

They heard the front door squeak as it opened. Elizabeth decided she would go to the stairs to try to stop him, or at least delay him from coming upstairs and getting to Larry and Ethel.

Arthur began wondering where they might be. He looked around the first floor a bit for any signs of their presence. He walked into the kitchen and to the basement door to listen for any noise.

He didn't hear anything. Then he heard a floor creak upstairs and decided they must be upstairs in the office. He knew the gun safe was in Frank's office. *He has an office upstairs just like Dad did*, Arthur thought. He figured they might be there.

Elizabeth quietly told Larry and Ethel to stay in the office and headed for the stairs.

"No, Mom, you can't go down there! He'll kill you!"

Elizabeth continued onward and reached the top of the steps.

Arthur looked up. "There you are."

"What did you do to your brother!" Elizabeth yelled.

"You'll see him soon enough."

"You stay down there, you son of a bitch! Elizabeth yelled."

He began slowly ascending the stairs, chuckling as he went.

Elizabeth waited for him at the top. "We have Frank's shotgun loaded and ready for you if you come any closer. I will blow your fucking head off!"

Arthur paused for a moment. He *thought if Elizabeth had the shotgun, she'd be carrying that instead of the bat. She probably wouldn't know how to load the shotgun even if she did have it. His mother might know how to load it, though, which slowed him down another step. His mother wouldn't shoot him, though, and Larry was a big chicken, just like he'd been at that age. And yet the boy had tried to fight him to protect Robert's girlfriend.*

As Arthur neared the top of the steps, Elizabeth ran back to the office and closed the door. She wondered whether Arthur would kill her since he'd killed Lexi. She believed he might but doubted he would kill Ethel or Larry. She wondered why he was here and what he was going to do.

Arthur walked down the hallway and approached the door. He tried the doorknob—locked. He jiggled the doorknob and then pushed on it. He knew he could easily ram the door and break it in. He liked scaring them.

"Arthur," Ethel yelled, "you need to stop and leave us alone. You can't hurt anyone else. Please stop this!"

"What did you do to Frank?" Elizabeth said. "He's your brother!"

Arthur rammed slightly into the door to scare them. Both of the women screamed. Arthur laughed.

"Oh yes, I can hurt everyone else, and I will until I die."

He pulled back and rammed the door harder, thinking it was sturdier than he'd initially thought. The door creaked with that push.

Jason had driven this route a few times lately, so he knew where they were going. At this point, they were about ten minutes from the Carols' house. There was one other police car behind them now as they flew through the Pennsylvania countryside.

Over the phone, Sheila told Michael, "We're on our way to the Carol house. We're about ten minutes away. Arthur's there, and he's trying to break into the room they're in."

Michael didn't bother telling them to wait for him because he knew they wouldn't. He explained he'd get there as soon as he could and that he knew Jason had called for backup.

"Please be careful," Michael added. "Arthur doesn't have anything to lose at this point, so he will kill anyone he can."

"We'll be as careful as we can be," Sheila said and hung up.

Arthur rammed the door hard three times before it broke away from the doorframe. He didn't step in right away, in case they'd planned to attack him. He pushed the door slowly open and peered into the room, where Elizabeth stood holding the baseball bat.

"That's a weird-looking shotgun," Arthur said and smiled, showing his yellowed and scraggly teeth.

Ethel immediately stepped in front of Elizabeth and Larry.

Arthur looked at his mom and did his deep chuckle. He stepped toward her and smiled.

"You killed Lexi!" Ethel said. "You are evil, and I am telling you—you can't hurt anyone else!"

Arthur quickly backhanded her hard across the face, and she stumbled backward and fell on a chair.

"After all I've done for you," she said, crying, "and you hit me like that."

"You should've left Dad and protected me!"

She stood and said, "We would've starved and had no place to go!"

Elizabeth held the bat as though she were about to hit a home run. She had played softball in high school and college. That was where she'd met Frank. She used this moment during which Arthur was distracted and ran toward him and swung the bat at his head. He raised his shoulder to protect his head, and the bat made contact with his gunshot wound, and he yelled in pain.

Elizabeth reloaded to strike him again. "You bastard, you killed my Lexi—your own niece! How could you do something like that? How could you kill any of these young women? You are sick!"

She swung the bat again and hit his forearm this time as he tried to deflect the blow. It still hurt, and he yelled again. Arthur finally seized the bat and pulled Elizabeth toward him. Arthur grabbed her and began choking her.

"I'm going to have sex with you," he said, "just like my mom used to with me. Mom and Larry are going to get to watch me fuck you."

At that moment, Larry ran up and started hitting Arthur in his wounded shoulder. Then he took hold of it and dug his fingers into the bullet hole, and Arthur screamed and shoved Larry away with his arm. Larry jumped right back on him and again dug his fingers in.

Arthur yelled and redirected his anger to Larry now. Arthur finally pulled his hammer out and hit Larry once in the chest, then turned to Elizabeth and aimed at her head, but missed.

Ethel picked up the baseball bat and quickly moved toward Arthur, hitting the hand wielding the hammer, causing Arthur to drop it. She then hit him on the back, and he yanked the bat from her hand.

Elizabeth crawled away from Arthur as he fought his mother. Larry fiercely yanked the bat out of Arthur's hand and hit him on his head, then his shoulder.

Arthur turned to Larry. "You should be like me! Your dad treated you like Grandpa treated me!"

Larry grit his teeth. "I'm not evil like you, and my dad's not perfect, but he's trying. You killed my sister, you bastard!"

Arthur walked toward Larry sternly and punched him in the head, knocking him down.

Ethel approached Arthur again. "Please don't hurt either of them any further! I'll go with you and take care of you."

"Fuck you!" Arthur said.

"Uncle Arthur," Larry said, "I'll go with you if you let them live."

Arthur quickly turned toward Larry and stared at him. Then he smiled. "One of them must die! Choose which one dies, and then we can leave."

"I can't do that!" Larry said. "If you let them both live, I'll go with you."

"Either you choose, or I'll choose."

"If one of us must die," Ethel said, walking toward Arthur, "then it should be me. I was the one who let your dad turn you into this monster."

Ethel touched Arthur's arm, and he turned and grabbed his mother by the neck and choked her very forcefully while looking into her eyes.

She didn't fight Arthur, only stared into his eyes as he choked her.

Arthur then picked up the hammer from the floor, and as he stared into Ethel's eyes, he struck her several times, quickly and hard.

"Awwwww!" he yelled. "You made me into this!"

Ethel bled a lot from the blows she was receiving from all his rage. Her head seemed to be caving in with such force. Tears began running down Arthur's face. Her eyes never closed, and she continued to stare into his eyes up to her death.

Arthur dropped her on the floor, and they all knew she was dead.

Larry and Elizabeth had stared at Ethel as this horror unfolded in front of them. They couldn't look away as Ethel's life slipped away.

Arthur then turned to Larry. "Now I'm done here. Boy, you need to go with me. Your dad was evil like my dad was. Your grandma is dead now too. She can't ruin you either. I shot your dad and killed him before I came in."

Larry and Elizabeth looked at Arthur silently as he said this.

At that moment, a voice came from behind Arthur.

"No you didn't—I'm not. You didn't kill me, but I told you I was going to kill you, and now it's time."

Arthur turned and raised the hammer as Frank Jr. walked through the door. He stumbled and leaned against the doorframe with a large bright pistol in his hand.

The front of Frank's body was very bloody from the two gunshot wounds. Arthur had a look of shock on his face as Frank began shooting him. The sound of the gunfire was incredibly loud in the room. Frank continued to shoot Arthur after he fell to the floor, until the gun was empty, and then Frank slid to the floor and dropped the gun.

CHAPTER 26

Jason saw the house, and two police cars were out front. One was close to the house, and the other was farther down the driveway, waiting. He wasn't sure what was going on and stopped by the car nearest to the street to assess the situation.

As they got out of their cars, they all listened in the darkness for any noises around them. The local police officer yelled out that he'd heard several gunshots right after he arrived and was waiting for backup. Jason had called in for backup telling them shots had been fired. They all pulled out their guns and began approaching the house.

Sheila and Jason slowly approached the door first to look inside. They had no idea what was happening in there at this point. Elizabeth's cell phone connection had dropped quite a while ago, and Robert hadn't received any more telepathic messages from Larry or Ethel.

Robert was suddenly drawn into a deep dark vision. He said, "Sheila!" right before it consumed him.

She turned to look at Robert and realized he had again entered into a death vision.

Robert saw Arthur shoot Frank Jr. and then enter the house. He then saw Arthur approach and begin up the stairs. He heard the exchange between the family members.

Sheila told Jason to be careful and go in, and she stayed with Robert through his vision. In the distance, she could hear more police cars approaching the house.

Robert entered the house and began up the stairs as he saw Arthur at the door and felt his anger, and even the fun he was having, as he frightened his remaining family. He saw Arthur break in the door and struggle with Elizabeth, Ethel, and Larry. He heard the dialogue as it had unfolded.

He witnessed Arthur grab his mother and murder her, and he'd enjoyed it yet cried. Just as Ethel fell to the floor, Robert came out of his vision. He was being held up by Sheila, and he turned and looked at her.

"Arthur killed Ethel," he said.

They were standing in the upstairs hallway looking in the door of Frank's office. Frank lay in the doorway.

Jason had approached the door ahead of them and yelled, "This is the police! We're coming in."

"We need an ambulance!" Elizabeth said. "We need help!"

Jason got on his mic and said, "We need an ambulance at the Carol house again right away."

When they got to the office door, Larry was kneeling down, applying pressure to his dad's chest. Elizabeth stood looking at them. Jason dropped down and checked Frank's vitals, and the family began relaying what had happened.

Jason picked up Frank's chrome nine-round Colt .357 Magnum revolver and passed it to the other officer, who handled it with gloves. When they entered the room, Ethel lay right next to Arthur on the floor. Arthur's eyes were wide open, looking at the ceiling, and he didn't move when they came in. Sheila went to him and saw all the bloody bullet marks on his chest and checked his neck for a pulse. There was none.

She turned her head and shook it, letting everyone know he was dead. She then walked over to Ethel, and though she felt it was unnecessary to check her pulse because of the damage that had been done, she did so regardless. She didn't bother letting them know this time.

Robert walked over to where Sheila was standing. In the distance they could hear the ambulance coming. Elizabeth cried and rested her hands on Larry's shoulders.

"Dad," Larry said, "the ambulance is almost here."

"Thanks, son," Frank said weakly.

The place was in utter chaos now as the police and EMTs came into the room.

Jason told the EMTs that Frank was in very serious condition and that the woman and the other man were deceased. The EMTs rightfully focused on Frank Jr. Lots of officers were talking and asking questions. Robert and Sheila went to Larry and Elizabeth as the EMTs placed Frank on a gurney and taped up his wounds so that he didn't bleed much more before he got to the hospital.

They skillfully took Frank on the gurney downstairs and out the door to the ambulance. It took them only about five minutes before the ambulance left. Elizabeth and Larry gladly agreed to be driven by police to the hospital. They held hands down to the police car and climbed in.

The CSU showed up to gather evidence about the crime scene and collected Arthur's and Ethel's bodies to transport them to the coroner's office for their autopsies.

Before the CSU was done, Robert, Sheila, Michael, and Jason went to the hospital to check on the Carol family. Frank was still in surgery when they arrived, but the doctor said he should be OK because the two bullets had missed all his vital organs.

Larry had been sleeping in the waiting area with his head on Elizabeth's lap when they arrived. Elizabeth and Larry got up and came to Sheila and Robert, and they all hugged one another. They remained there for a while and let Elizabeth and Larry explain to them what had happened.

"We don't know how we would have survived without the two of you!" Elizabeth said. "Thank you so much."

Larry shook Robert's hand and hugged Sheila.

Robert and Sheila both told Larry they were proud of him and how strong he'd been through all the bad things his uncle Arthur did, and he thanked them.

Before Robert and Sheila left the hospital, Michael approached them and told them he was so glad they'd helped him out so much. He told them to go home and get some sleep and then come to the police station later that day.

It was early in the morning when Jason drove them to Sheila's house. Robert thanked Jason for everything as he was about to leave.

"Thank God this is all over," Jason said, "and he won't be able to kill anyone else. I'm going to go home and go to bed."

They shook hands, and Jason said they would talk later. Sheila and Robert just wanted to eat and get some sleep. They went in and made a couple of ham-and-cheese sandwiches before lying down in Sheila's bed and falling asleep in each other's arms.

After Sheila and Robert woke, they ate, got ready, and climbed into the Jeep to head to the police station.

"The police haven't identified all the victims at this point," Michael said, "and now they have the two older cases of the women at the cabin who Frank Sr. killed. Wish us luck!

"I've talked to the DA, and none of the remaining family will be charged with anything because they didn't know what was going on with Arthur. This was all Arthur, and he showed many of the signs of psychopathy. The environment he grew up in with his parents didn't cause this, but it didn't help him. It made it worse or reinforced it.

"The coroner sent us a photo of Arthur's shot pattern in his torso, and it was a pretty close pattern of shots—they believe he died immediately, maybe even before he hit the floor. He knew his time was coming. The coroner also found some of the women's trophies in two of Arthur's pockets and assorted hair in another. We also made sure the hammer and knife went to the coroner with Arthur."

"We assumed we would find his serial killer trophies at the old Carol house and didn't. He kept the trophies with him."

Serials usually had a hidden place where they stored trophies they collected from their victims.

Robert and Sheila phoned Mr. White to schedule one last meeting with the families to give them the final details. Robert went into the spare bedroom and began writing more or less a summary of everything to close this out for them. Of course, such tragedies never went away. The survivors would remember their lost family members sadly forever.

It took Robert another day to write it up and draw what had

happened. *I'm so glad I took this job*, he thought. *I certainly affected the outcome with my gift*. But there was still a lot of story to tell, and he would fill in the gaps.

They left the next day open to meet, and that morning, they got up and ate breakfast before they drove to Mr. White's house. They stopped at the library on the way and made copies. The same librarian was once again watching every move, curious about what they were doing. Robert and Sheila just smiled and waved at her.

They drove to the Whites' house, and Mr. White met them at the door. He told them everyone would be there today to finish it out. He grabbed and shook Robert's hand, then Sheila's.

"I want to thank you both so much for helping solve this for us and get some closure," Mr. White said.

"You all need to take some of the credit," Robert said. "If you hadn't trusted your instincts and pulled this all together, he would still be out there."

They waited for a little while to begin. Robert and Sheila stood by the fireplace, and different members of each family walked up and talked to them. This was the largest group so far, and the mood in the room seemed better than usual.

Mr. White finally asked everyone to take a seat.

"Mr. Anderson and Ms. Flores are with us one last time," he said. "I know I personally can't thank them enough for helping prove that the police had the wrong person for these crimes. Then they decided to help finish this up, which they didn't have to do.

"I'm going to give them a check to show my gratitude for everything they've done, putting their very lives on the line to bring this nightmare to an end. Mr. Anderson, we knew we had to do something, and, Ms. Flores, thank you so much for working together and doing this for us. We're sure that even though you couldn't do anything to bring our young women back, you did stop this madman from killing even more. You're our heroes!"

At that, the entire room broke out in applause.

"If you could go through your final death journal with us," Mr. White said, "we can conclude this."

"I'm very happy that you figured out that the police had it wrong,"

Robert said, "and reached out to Sheila and me, because you are the heroes here. You are the people who made this happen."

He looked at Sheila, who was smiling from ear to ear.

"That being said," Robert continued, "Sheila and I will begin going through this final journal, and hopefully you'll never need us again."

Sheila started the journal off, and they took turns reading and explaining the events that had taken place that they hadn't yet shared with the families. A few people cried during the journal reading, and Robert and Sheila were both considerate of the mood of the room.

Everyone once again cheered when Robert and Sheila concluded with what they'd most recently learned from Michael at the police station.

Robert thought back on his grandma telling him that his gift had been given to him to help people, and that's what he would do going forward—and hopefully Sheila would work alongside him.

Robert and Sheila did receive a generous amount of money from the families for their help, but they weren't sure what they were going to do with it. Alberto Black didn't attend the last meeting.

They went to Sheila's house and began to relax for a few days of detox before figuring out what to do next together. They'd been sitting on the couch for a bit, watching TV, snacking, and drinking some wine.

Suddenly Sheila asked, "So how do you feel about us?"

"You know," Robert said, "I believe I'm falling in love with you. I love every moment we're together."

"I feel the very same way," Sheila said, "even outside of us working together. I believe I'm falling in love with you too!"

They began hugging and kissing, which led to their touching each other, and before they knew it, they were removing each other's clothes. Robert laid Sheila back on the couch and began kissing her all over her body. He focused on areas of her body that she seemed sensitive to her. She loved her toes receiving his attention for some reason. After she had orgasmed a couple of times, she pushed Robert back on the couch and began at his neck, then moved down to his nipples and belly button. He didn't like his toes being licked or sucked because he was ticklish. He did very much enjoy her mouth on him and he was ready when she climbed on top of him and they were joined. She began riding him slowly, and the pace increased until they both had one final orgasm and collapsed on the couch, where they kissed and held each other again.

The next day, Sheila was on her computer reviewing some email messages she'd received while the madness was going on. Her doorbell rang, and she went to see who it was. She opened the door to a smiling young man.

"Are you Sheila Flores?" he asked.

"Yes, I am. What's going on?"

He handed her a set of car keys. "These are for you."

He waved his hand at a new Mercedes S600 parked in the driveway. Then he handed her an envelope and turned and walked away.

Robert came to the door. "So what's going on?"

"I don't know yet," Sheila replied, "but he told me the Mercedes in the driveway is mine. Let's go read this."

They settled on the couch, and Sheila opened the envelope, which included the title for the Mercedes and a note:

> I learned that your car was destroyed by Mr. Carol, and you're going to need a car to help with the work you'll be doing with my group, so I bought this for you. You and Robert take a break, and then I'm going to put you to work. Tell Robert to call his mother. She's worried about him.
>
> Sincerely,
> Alberto Black

Another of his business cards was enclosed. Robert and Sheila were stunned.

The went out and went for a short drive in her new car. It was a convertible too. When they returned, Robert called his family that afternoon, and he and Sheila promised they would drive her new car to Cincinnati that weekend.

It was a nice drive to Cincinnati in Sheila's new Mercedes. Robert's family had all gathered together to congratulate the two of them for solving the crimes, and they were all eager to meet Sheila.

Robert and Sheila remained there for a couple of days to make the family feel better. Robert's mother made up a room with a queen-size bed for them to stay in, which was very nice. They told the family about Mr. Black wanting to hire them for some special team he was forming to help people.

His mother pulled him aside and said that she really liked Sheila and they seemed very compatible.

"I care about her a lot," Robert said, "and I think we're in love with each other. We literally saved each other's lives over the past two weeks."

"I've talked to some folks I know from Kentucky who knew about your and Grandma's special gift," his mother said, "and they told me about one person who seemed to have your gift too."

She was going to try to dig a little deeper to get in touch with that person, and she would let him know when she had.

When they left for Sheila's house, it was rainy, with periodic thundershowers almost the entire drive back. They felt they should go visit Sheila's family again soon to touch base. Both of them were pretty close to their families.

They talked about what they should do next. Her neighbors were beginning to reach out to her about their moving since so much drama had occurred during the recent activities involving Arthur Lee Carol.

Maybe they needed to find something close to one of her cop brothers, at least temporarily. She wasn't devoted to her house or its location. They did enjoy spending time hiking close to Sheila's house, though, and they could set up her second bedroom as an office.

Three weeks after Arthur and Ethel Carol died, Frank Jr. had recovered fairly well from his shots, and he, Larry, and Elizabeth were attending counseling to help recover from their awful ordeal and to improve Frank's relationship with both of them. They were finally able to get Lexi's body back for her funeral. Now they had to bury Ethel and Arthur too. They would have separate services for them. Actually, they would just have Arthur buried, but in the same cemetery.

Frank did tell Elizabeth about the secretary who'd been giving oral sex him, like she had his father.

Frank threw himself on his sword, telling her, "I knew it was wrong the entire time and didn't stop her. I thought since my father did it, it might be OK, but I knew it wasn't."

She didn't love it, and didn't talk to him about it for a day, but they seemed to be doing better. This didn't bother Elizabeth as much as it maybe should have. Frank was getting more involved in Larry's life. Elizabeth stayed in touch with Sheila. She told Sheila everything, including that they were considering going on a lengthy vacation to try to rebuild their lives together.

Later that evening, if either Robert or Sheila had looked out the front window, they might have seen the dark car with blacked-out windows that was sitting a short distance away, waiting and watching.

She wasn't sure just what she hoped to gain or learn from sitting here. She'd read the news and seen the stories on television, so she knew what Robert was capable of. She'd been told by Mr. Black that they might be working together sometime soon. She wondered whether he could help her with her problem. She guessed she'd find out soon.

EPILOGUE

When Robert and Sheila called Mr. Black, he wanted them to come to one of his offices for a meeting soon. He'd inherited a great deal of money from his parents and then learned how to invest it very well. He felt like he really needed to use his wealth to help people, especially victims. He'd lost a sister when they were young to violent crime, and it affected the rest of his life and set him on this path.

He thought the best way he could help people was to identify a group of people with complementary skills, and they could try to work with law enforcement and federal agencies to combat these serious crime problems—although many law enforcement and feds weren't eager to do this, and they were many times prevented from reciprocating information.

Law enforcement had come a long way in sharing information since the 1980s, when the serial killer crime wave occurred in the United States, but they could still use some help. Mr. Black had already established the group who would perform all the research and data analysis, as well as a custom system that had connections to other government and police systems that identified and tracked crime and criminals. They could access fingerprints, DNA, missing persons, biometric data, and criminal tracking, including serious registered criminals who got released from prisons or sanitoriums. As other new systems came online, he would pay to gain access to them as well.

He was now also trying to locate team members such as Robert Anderson who had special knowledge, experience, and now even paranormal capabilities that would allow him to look outside the box with his team.

To begin with, he hoped they could make a huge difference with any criminal activity that appeared to be escalating around the country and in Canada. The crimes were beyond psychopathic activity. It was about evil greed and power.

Mr. Black was afraid it looked like the serial killer activity that had peaked during the late '70s and '80s was beginning to ramp up again. Serial killers were psychopaths but not idiots, and many had learned what they needed to do to prevent discovery. Many of them had charm and high IQs. They prey on the weak, outcasts, and the helpless. Despite the fact that DNA identification was now available, that technology helped only once a crime had occurred. His operation would help them much more, but many times, the police didn't even realize it was a serial until the person had killed four or five people. He felt it was extremely important to have Robert, who could paranormally see what the victims saw, get to a crime scene right after it happened. There were others Mr. Black was trying to identify and locate who had other types of abilities and experience.

When Robert and Sheila came to his office, Mr. Black began by asking them how they liked the car.

"It's nicer than what I'm used to," Sheila said, "but I love it! Thank you!"

Mr. Black looked at Robert and asked whether he'd recovered from the Carol killings—or really all the killings.

"Yes, I'm doing much better now," Robert said. "I'm not sure I'll ever forget how awful that situation was."

Sheila asked some questions about what Mr. Black was trying to accomplish and how they could help. He told them how he felt they could join his team, and he explained who was on his team so far and what they could do. The two of them would be a great addition, and he was considering some other people with other special skills and experience.

Mr. Black walked Robert and Sheila around the offices and introduced them to the inside members of the team. He then took them into the computer server room so they could see he was seriously invested in this. He told them he owned a couple of helicopters and a private jet.

"I have a half dozen more cases you could work on, so let me know when you're ready."

He also told them his idea of rushing them to locations where recent criminal deaths had occurred in which the suspect might be serial in nature. He told them how much he was willing to pay them, and they were happy. At the end of the day, they got in the new Mercedes and drove back to Sheila's house to prepare for their next case. Robert now had a good job surprisingly based on his Paranormal abilities and a beautiful woman he loved. Things were falling into place. Their relationship was continuing to build as they got to know each other better. Robert wondered what their future together would look like working with others with special skills and what skills each of them might have.

Alberto Black began to see his vision begin to come together and how these special people would work with each other and solve some of these crimes.

Printed in the USA
CPSIA information can be obtained
at www.ICGtesting.com
CBHW031942080424
6607CB00001B/72